"The things th___ tonight, Harry___ I no longer fee___ you. And I do ___ ___ I'm tired of pretending I don't. I want to spend the night with you."

He tried to wrestle the temptation back under control. "Two things," he ground out.

She folded her arms. "Okay."

"We're not spending tonight together."

Her face fell.

"If you were to regret it in the morning, I'd feel like a heel. You're vulnerable right now. I can't take advantage of that."

"While I think you're wrong, I don't want to make love with you if you're worried about that."

Damn, he liked this woman.

"And the second thing?" she asked.

"The wedding."

"If word was to get out that you and I had..."

"And we don't want to do anything—"

"To ruin the wedding," she finished.

He took a step toward her. Her eyes widened and the pulse in her throat fluttered like a wild thing. It took all of his strength not to press a kiss there.

Dear Reader,

I was recently feeling wistful that I hadn't been to a wedding in more than two years. So I did what any good writer does: I decided to attend one of my own making...through the pages of a book.

Enter Ella and Harry, the bridesmaid and best man for said wedding. They become friends at first sight, but there are *so* many reasons they can't be more than that. Of course, weddings rarely go exactly as planned—a lot like life, in fact. Ella and Harry's machinations to save this wedding coupled with their attempts to ignore the attraction building between them kept me on the edge of my seat as I wrote the story.

"But you're the author," I hear you say. "You should know what's going to happen." Well, apparently, Dear Reader, writing a book is a lot like weddings and a lot like life. Sometimes it doesn't go to plan. And sometimes that makes life, and books, richer and more authentic. I hope you find yourself cheering Ella and Harry on as much as I did as they try to save both a wedding and themselves.

Hugs and happy reading!

Michelle

Wedding Date in Malaysia

Michelle Douglas

—

HARLEQUIN

Romance

Recycling programs
for this product may
not exist in your area.

ISBN-13: 978-1-335-40713-9

Wedding Date in Malaysia

Copyright © 2022 by Michelle Douglas

For questions and comments about the quality of this book, please contact us at CustomerService@Harlequin.com.

Harlequin Enterprises ULC
22 Adelaide St. West, 41st Floor
Toronto, Ontario M5H 4E3, Canada
www.Harlequin.com

Printed in U.S.A.

Michelle Douglas has been writing for Harlequin since 2007 and believes she has the best job in the world. She lives in a leafy suburb of Newcastle, on Australia's east coast, with her own romantic hero, a house full of dust and books, and an eclectic collection of '60s and '70s vinyl. She loves to hear from readers and can be contacted via her website, michelle-douglas.com.

Books by Michelle Douglas

Harlequin Romance

A Baby in His In-Tray
The Million Pound Marriage Deal
Miss Prim's Greek Island Fling
The Maid, the Millionaire and the Baby
Redemption of the Maverick Millionaire
Singapore Fling with the Millionaire
Secret Billionaire on Her Doorstep
Billionaire's Road Trip to Forever
Cinderella and the Brooding Billionaire
Escape with Her Greek Tycoon

Visit the Author Profile page
at Harlequin.com for more titles.

To Newcastle Romance Writers, for the monthly meetings and the weekly sprints, but mostly for the fun and fellowship. Oh, and the wine.

Praise for
Michelle Douglas

CHAPTER ONE

'RIGHT, SO I haven't told you about the brides-maid yet.'

Harry raised an eyebrow as Martin concen-trated on reversing his four-by-four into one of the restaurant's parking bays. What was wrong with the bridesmaid?

Was she some predatory gold-digger? Or worse still a party girl? He glanced at the harbour twin-kling with a thousand lights—like a party!—and winced. Being linked with a woman like that at the moment wouldn't do his image makeover any good.

When Martin didn't continue, even after switching off the engine, Harry's gut clenched, but he pushed his shoulders back. He had every inten-tion of taking his best man duties seriously, even if that included dealing with a difficult Bridezilla of a bridesmaid.

Though, could a bridesmaid technically be a Bridezilla? That term, by definition, belonged to the bride, didn't it?

Oh, for God's sake, Harrison, concentrate.

'C'mon, spit it out. Why'd you say "the brides-maid" like that? As if it was in italics or some-thing?'

He needed to know what he was up against. Agreeing to be Martin's best man was supposedly step one in Operation New Leaf. He needed to convince the world—or at least the trustees of the charity he wanted to partner with—that he was a changed man who'd given up his playboy ways.

Playboy ways that weren't entirely earned, he reminded himself.

Earned or not, it didn't change the fact that he had the kind of *reputation* entirely deserving of italics.

'You're taking a long time answering the ques-tion, Martin.' It wasn't setting his mind at rest.

'I'm just trying to think of the most tactful way of putting it.'

This was going from bad to worse!

Hold on... 'I've met Susie.' He'd met Martin's intended yesterday when he'd flown in from Swit-zerland. 'She's a sweetheart.' Which was true. 'I can't imagine her having a gorgon of a girlfriend, let alone choosing someone like that to be her bridesmaid.'

'Oh, Ellie isn't a gorgon. She's just…sad.'

He eased back to stare at Martin. *Sad?*

'She's the one who was engaged to Susie's brother.'

He wracked his brain. Susie's brother…?

Martin rolled his eyes. 'You're jet-lagged.'

Considering he'd only flown in yesterday from the other side of the world, he didn't feel too bad. But he had been burning the candle at both ends lately. Though *not* in the way the tabloids would suggest. He'd had a lot on his mind, but he'd have to switch gears now he was back in Australia—for both Martin's sake and the sake of Operation New Leaf.

'James died… I guess it'd be over twelve months ago now.'

He slapped a hand to his head. 'Drowned. Great guy. Awful tragedy.'

'That's the one.'

'Aw, c'mon, Martin, put yourself in her shoes.'

'I know! I know! And I don't mean to sound unsympathetic, but she's the maid of honour, for God's sake. Is it really too much to ask her to put on a brave face and be happy for Susie?'

He grimaced. His friend had a point.

'She's bringing down the whole tone of the celebrations. It's like no one can be too happy or festive around her. This is supposed be one of the happiest times of my life—*of Susie's life*—something we remember forever. Instead, it's turning into a wake.'

Harry shifted on his seat. 'Why the hell did Susie ask her, then? And if she's grieving—' if she'd been in the process of planning her own wedding '—why on earth did this Ellie agree to be Susie's bridesmaid?'

Martin raised his hands, a mystified expression on his face. 'I'm all ears if you can explain to me why women do what they do, why they make the decisions they make, when those decisions seem to defy logic. When I asked her why she chose her, Susie said, "Because it's the right thing to do." Right thing for who? That's what I want to know.'

Harry let out a slow breath. He of all people knew how difficult relationships could be.

Not romantic relationships, though. He avoided those like the plague.

'The two families are close. Susie's mum and Ellie's mum have been best friends since kindergarten. And once they married, the two couples went into business together. So Susie and Ellie grew up together. They're more like sisters than friends.'

The word sister had his gut clenching. If Susie and this Ellie were that close then they'd probably do anything for each other, regardless of the cost to themselves. That was something he understood.

'So this is where you come in, Harrison.'

He snapped to attention. 'Me?'

'I want you to do everything in your power to cheer her up, to get her to loosen up and enter into the spirit of the thing.'

What?

'You're good at getting people to laugh and

let their hair down. Nobody throws a party like you do.'

Hell. He was supposed to be shedding the Harrison 'party boy, bad boy, can't-be-serious-for-a-moment' routine. He dragged a hand down his face. God, he was so typecast.

And whose fault is that?

He'd hoped acting as Martin's best man would help him present a more responsible image to the world, not reinforce his current one.

'But I *only* want you to cheer her up. Save any other shenanigans for some other girl, all right?'

He glanced at Martin. Was he asking him to just *platonically* cheer her up?

'No hanky-panky with the bridesmaid unless—' Martin bumped shoulders with him '—you've changed your view on relationships. It comes to all of us, you know?'

That was an out-and-out lie, but he didn't bother challenging him on it. For God's sake, the man was marrying the woman of his dreams in three months. He obviously believed in true love and happy-ever-afters. But for some people that kind of long-term commitment didn't stick, the ability to go the long haul wasn't in their make-up. 'Nope, no change on that front.'

'Ellie's a hearts-and-roses kind of girl. She and James were childhood sweethearts. They'd never dated anyone else.'

Seriously?

'I wouldn't like to see her get hurt.'

He raised both hands. 'Definitely not my type. I run a mile from women like that. Best behaviour,' he promised.

'Besides,' Martin added, 'it'd cause a bit of an uproar.'

What did that mean?

'I'm relying on you, Harrison. I don't want any drama marring my wedding.' He leapt out of the car. 'Ready?'

'Ready,' he agreed, pushing out of the car.

Martin and Susie had booked out a restaurant with stunning views of Sydney harbour. They'd wanted all the interested parties—families, close friends, and wedding attendants—to meet each other before the big day.

The restaurant was small, which made it feel crowded, and it looked as if he and Martin were the last to arrive. And despite what Martin had said, the atmosphere was convivial.

He met Susie's parents and chatted with Martin's—who asked after his mother, though not his father—and a few of the couple's nearest and dearest before Martin bustled him over to a woman in the middle of a group of other women.

'Ellie, I'd like you to meet my best man, Harrison Gillespie. Harrison, this is Ellie Hawthorne.'

He found himself staring down into the brightest blue eyes he'd ever seen. They smiled into his as she held out her hand. 'It's lovely to meet you,

Harrison. I've heard a lot about you.' She rolled her eyes at Martin. 'And I'm El*la*.' She stressed the second syllable.

He took her hand and found himself encompassed in warmth and...welcome. He frowned. She made him feel *welcome*. He couldn't work out how. Or why he wanted to rest in that welcome, put up his feet and just...be.

He shook himself. Jet lag, he must have it bad this time around. 'I'm pleased to meet you too, El*la*.' He stressed the second syllable in the same fashion she did, which made her eyes dance.

'You don't have a drink. Let's remedy that.'

She smiled and he immediately relaxed. Ella's entire demeanour calmed any concerns he might've had. Her expression was the same as the one that the women who always avoided him wore—the ones who dismissed him as frivolous and not to be trusted with their hearts—determinedly friendly but determinedly distant too.

Ella couldn't currently avoid him so she was doing the next best thing—putting him firmly in the friend zone. He *loved* the friend zone.

'Susie is trying to get your attention, Martin. Leave Harrison with me.' Ella took Harry's arm. 'He's in safe hands.' She turned to the assorted throng around her. 'You'll have to excuse us,' she said. 'We have important bridesmaid and best man business to discuss.'

Her hand on his arm tightened and he went on

immediate high alert. Whenever Lily seized his arm like that, it meant she needed rescuing. Who the hell was hassling Ella?

He hated men who preyed on vulnerable women. He'd be more than happy to set the guilty party straight.

He searched the vicinity as she led him towards the bar, but couldn't find a likely suspect. He frowned. Perhaps her covert urgency had another cause. 'Do we have important bridesmaid and best man business to discuss?' Was there something he needed to do, a problem he needed to solve or—?

'Oh, I don't know. Probably.'

She shrugged without looking at him and continued towards the bar. She had short dark curls that danced as she walked—glossy, shiny and the colour of the icing on a chocolate éclair.

The thought made him blink. He couldn't remember the last time he'd eaten anything sweet and sticky. He wasn't much into desserts, but if someone set a chocolate éclair in front of him now, he'd wolf it down and relish every bite.

He frowned. She was nothing like he'd expected. After Martin's description, he'd pictured a pale waif with tragic eyes brimming with tears, and a general air of inertia. Not this lively woman who moved with brisk purpose.

She sent him a smile as she slid up onto a stool.

'If the truth be told, I just needed a little break from the gathering horde.'

Her smile removed any sting from the words and he suddenly realised that she no longer held his arm, although the imprint of her fingers continued to burn on his flesh. It occurred to him then that her former touch had been mercifully brief.

Or do you mean mercilessly?

The thought made him swallow.

'I mean, I love them dearly, don't get me wrong, but they can be a bit much en masse.'

Hold on, she'd been desperate to get away from…

He glanced back the way they'd come and found a large proportion of the room sending covert glances Ella's way—biting lips, shaking heads and heaving sighs.

He turned back to Ella, who wasn't looking at him but studying the wine list. She'd been desperate to get away from all of that commiseration and *pity*? Pursing his lips, he nodded. He supposed it must get a bit suffocating after a while.

She clapped the wine list shut. 'What'll you have?'

'A beer.'

'Would you like to try one of these new-fangled craft beers?'

He really didn't care and she interpreted his shrug as such because she didn't ask any other questions, merely pointed to one of the beers on tap and ordered a glass of white wine for herself.

'So…you prefer Ella?'

'I do. Not that anyone pays the slightest bit of attention.' There was the tiniest edge to her words, but before he could attempt to decipher what that meant, she sent him another of those discombobulating smiles. 'And you prefer Harrison?'

Actually, he didn't. 'I like Harry, but my parents insisted on calling me Harrison and, therefore, so did the teachers at school. And therefore so did all the kids at school.'

Their glasses were set in front of them and she raised hers to clink it with his. 'Harry it is, then.'

And something inside him unwound. Just like that. Something that felt as if it had been wound tight his whole life.

'So…'

She leaned towards him and he wondered if he'd read her incorrectly and that maybe she was about to start flirting with him.

'Do you know what Martin and—?'

A middle-aged man clamped a hand to Ella's arm, and her words stuttered to a halt. 'How are you doing, Ellie dear?'

'I'm well, Uncle Aubrey, and you?'

'It's nice to see you making such an effort for our dear Susie's sake.'

'Well, I'm very happy for Susie, and this *is* a night of celebration.'

'Och, you're a good lass.'

Uncle Aubrey patted Ella's hand as if… Harry blinked. As if she were a sad puppy!

'You're doing your parents proud.'

And then he left, and Ella turned back to the bar and gulped wine, avoiding Harry's gaze. 'That was Uncle Aubrey, who's actually Susie's dad's second cousin, so not really an uncle at all, but you know how these things are. I'd have introduced you, but…'

'He didn't really give you the chance.'

She straightened. 'So what I was going to ask was, has Martin let anything slip about…?'

Her gaze moved to a point behind his right shoulder and her words trailed off again. He swung around to find a slender woman standing there, staring at Ella with tears in her eyes.

'Hello, Adele, how are you?'

Tears fell. 'Oh, Ellie, I don't know how you can stand it. When you should be here with…well, you know.'

He found himself wanting to shout, *Her name is Ella, not Ellie!*

'No, no, don't mind me.' Adele dabbed at her eyes with a tissue. 'I'll just—'

'Oh, no you don't.' Ella slid off her stool, wrapped an arm around the other woman's shoulders and steered her to a seat between both of them. 'You're not crying on Susie's shoulder. Not tonight. Tonight is a happy night. Have you met Harry yet? He's Martin's best man.'

The tears dried up. 'Best man? Oh! So he's not your date?'

For a moment he wished he were so he could wipe the relief from this woman's face.

'We were just having a best man and brides-maid confab.'

'Oh, then I won't interrupt.'

With that she leapt up and disappeared back into the crowd. The nosy so-and-so. She'd just wanted to find out who the hell he was.

Ella stared into her glass with pursed lips. She had pretty lips, but it was the curl resting against one dusky cheek that caught his attention. No matter how much he might want to, he couldn't reach out and wind it around his finger, and—

Stop it!

He rolled his shoulders. Old habits and all that. He just hadn't realised how ingrained they were. He was *not* going to flirt with Ella Hawthorne. He wasn't flirting with *any* woman.

Ella pulled in a big breath that made her chest rise. He averted his gaze and refused to notice *anything*. He especially wasn't going to notice the sweet curve of her chest.

'Okay, let's get the elephant in the room out of the way.' Resentment lurked in the back of those blue eyes, but he didn't think it was directed at him. 'Have you heard about James yet?'

With someone else he might've hemmed and hawed, treaded softly, but he sensed she'd prefer straight talk. He went with his gut and nodded. 'Susie's brother who died over a year ago.'

Her lips twisted. 'Eighteen months.'

That was a year and a half. 'And you were engaged to him.'

'That's right.'

He stared at her for a long moment. 'So how are you really doing?'

She stared back, her eyes not wavering from his. 'Actually, I'm doing really well.'

He believed her.

And then he frowned. From where he was sitting, Ella was doing a fine job of putting on a brave face. What was Martin's problem?

'Ellie, dear.' An elderly woman came bustling up on his other side.

Ella pasted on a bright smile. 'Have you met Harry yet, Aunt Edith?'

She introduced him as Harry rather than Harrison and he found himself absurdly touched.

'Susie's grandmother on her mum's side is one of five sisters and Edith here is the eldest.' Her smile widened. 'You can imagine what Christmas dinner is like, can't you?'

He recognised her pre-empt attempt at diversion—trying to get in before she became an object of pity and subjected to yet more platitudes. He sensed her quiet desperation returning. It didn't show in her face, but he saw the way her fingers tightened around her wine glass in the same way they'd tightened on his arm earlier.

It occurred to him then that Ella was close to her breaking point. If someone didn't do something soon, she could go off like a firecracker. If she did, Martin and Susie's celebrations would be remembered for all the wrong reasons.

And Ella would hate herself forever.

He didn't know how he knew that, only that he did. And he couldn't let it happen. He leapt into the breach. 'Five sisters? I'm guessing Christmas is rowdy. Really rowdy. And fun.' He thrust his hand out towards the older woman. 'It's nice to meet you.'

Edith frowned. 'I…'

'Are you ladies on the blue lagoons already? Way to go!' Ella leaned closer as she held up a hand to high-five the other woman and her scent—all peachy freshness—dredged his senses. 'It's clearly going to be a good night.'

She had the kind of smile that could fell a man. Not to mention gumption. She was digging deep to keep up this front. He was determined to do whatever he could to help her.

Edith heaved a gusty sigh. 'You don't need to put a brave face on for us, Ellie. We understand what you're going through. Dinner is about to be served and we've saved you a seat at our table. We don't want you feeling lonely. We widows need to stick together.'

He felt Ella flinch and in that moment he saw it all. It wasn't that Ella was so sad—it was that everyone else still was. And they were projecting it all onto her.

Damn it all to hell.

His hands clenched and unclenched, even as his heart went out to not just Ella but everyone else as well. They probably didn't know they were doing it. But trying to keep James alive through Ella—martyring her on some awful altar of remembrance—wasn't fair. It made him want to…

He rolled his shoulders. He wasn't sure. But he wanted to do something.

Ella's strength, though, astounded him. She kept her chin high, she kept the smile on her face. 'That's very thoughtful of you, Edith.'

She'd pushed all of that boiling bubbling frustration and desperation back deep down, and he winced. That couldn't be good for her.

'We're looking forward to hearing all your news, Ellie love, and talking about old times.'

Dear God. He might not be able to do anything else, but he could at least rescue her from a dreary night spent on the *widows' table*.

'I'm sorry, Edith, but I've already claimed Ella for the evening. As best man and bridesmaid we obviously have important wedding business to discuss.'

* * *

Ella had to fight an entirely inappropriate laugh at the shock on Aunt Edith's face.

'But perhaps after dessert we can join your table for a...'

He glanced towards Edith's table and the jug of bright blue cocktail sitting there, and she swore she heard him swallow, which had her fighting another laugh.

'...for a drink. I'd like to meet all of Susie's family.'

Edith hefted up her ample bosom as if to challenge him, but before she could splutter out an argument, Harry slid from his stool and took Ella's hand to help her down from hers. 'You'll have to excuse us, but Martin and Susie must be wondering where we've got to.'

He didn't drop Ella's hand as she'd expected, but led her away from Susie's flabbergasted great-aunt towards the table where Susie and Martin sat with their parents. Ella glanced back at Edith with a smile and a shrug, but it didn't stop the guilt from rolling through her.

Edith and her sisters had loved James so very much. She understood how much they missed him. She missed him too, but—

'How can you stand it?'

Harry lowered his head to murmur the question in her ear and it stirred the hair at her temples, sending prickles along her nape and raising the fine hairs on her arms. She didn't know if that was the result of the question he'd asked or the effect of the man himself.

Not that she had any intention of taking Harry Gillespie seriously. She'd heard all about his reputation, thank you very much. She had no intention of falling victim to his playboy charm. She wasn't falling for *anyone's* charm, playboy or otherwise. She barely managed to suppress a shudder at the thought.

Before she'd managed to formulate a response to his question, though, they were standing at Susie and Martin's table.

'You're joining us?' Susie's eyebrows rose and her teeth worried her bottom lip.

Ella bit back a sigh. She truly was the black widow—the kiss of death to all fun and frivolity. No wonder Edith had tried dragging her off to the *widows' table*. It wasn't that she was trying to prevent Ella from feeling lonely. It was that she didn't want Ella raining on anyone else's parade.

If they'd only give her half a chance, she'd show them that she could be the life and soul.

Well, you know how to fix that. Return to the fold—

She flinched at the thought. Tried to cut it dead. Couldn't face it. If she surrendered her dream now, she couldn't help feeling it would be the slow death of who she was.

Except following her dream was making everyone else unhappy!

Maybe they were right. Maybe she was being reckless and selfish. She was so tired of being on the outer, of constantly having to justify her choices...of being the source of so much worry. James's death had hurt everyone so badly. Did she really have it in her to keep hurting them?

She suddenly realised she had a death grip on Harry's hand and loosened her hold. Her eyes burned, but she forced up her chin. Next week. She'd tell them next week. Monday. She'd say she'd made a mistake, would return to the family business...and to a life of dull, secure monotony.

But deep inside her a voice whispered that she shouldn't have to surrender all her dreams simply to make everyone else happy.

'Auntie Edith told me she was organising for you to sit with them.'

Had there been phone calls prior to this evening's gathering about how best to handle Ella? She'd bet there had been. Why couldn't they acknowledge that she was making an effort? They'd all lost James. Not just her.

Pulling in a breath, she let it out slowly. She knew how much they were hurting, and she'd do anything she could to change that. But it was as if whenever she was in the room the family didn't see her any more, all they could see was James's absence.

She was trying to do her best by and for Susie. Why couldn't Susie return the favour? Unlike Ella, the family was letting *her* move on. Didn't she have it in her to extend some of that grace to Ella? Rather than relegating her to the *widows' table*?

Ella did what she could to beat down the resentment. Susie had idolised James. Losing him had blown her world apart. It had blown all their worlds apart. In the grand scheme of things sitting with the great-aunts was a small sacrifice to make. And if she was honest she couldn't care less where she sat.

So why the pang at the thought of not sitting with Harry?

Because, for all his playboy ways, he was a breath of fresh air. In the same way anyone who hadn't known James would be a breath of fresh air.

She opened her mouth to say she'd go and sit with Edith, but Harry spoke first. 'Susie, your bridesmaid is too young to be banished to the great-aunts' table.'

It felt odd to have someone going into bat for her. Odd but nice.

His mouth hooked up in a crooked grin and she saw the charm that must've won him at least a thousand hearts over the years. 'That said, I can see you and Ella making up your own great-aunts' table in another fifty years and getting up to all sorts of shenanigans.'

Just for a moment Susie's eyes met hers and they shared a grin—a 'before James had died' kind of grin. Ella pointed at her. 'We are *not* drinking blue lagoons.'

'What will we drink instead?' Susie asked.

'Champagne, of course. We'll be on the bubbles, darling.'

But the smile had already started to fade from Susie's face. It was the same with everyone. They'd enjoy a brief moment with her, and then feel guilty because James was no longer here. In this instance, though, Susie's smile became a frown. Her gaze lowered, and with a start Ella realised that her and Harry's hands were still linked.

'Mind you—' Harry craned his neck towards Edith's table '—they've just ordered another jug of blue lagoon. *That* could be the party table. You up for it, Ella?'

Her cheeks burned and she tugged her hand free. She hadn't realised she'd left her hand in his. It'd just been so nice to let someone else take charge for a moment that she'd let herself wallow in it.

Dangerous.

It struck her then how tired she was. Which meant she was getting closer and closer to her breaking point. And she had to guard against that with everything she had.

Martin shot to his feet. 'Of course you should sit with us.' He gestured to the spare seats at the end of the table, but he didn't meet Ella's eye. He never met her eye.

Wine was poured and the conversations continued around them, but nobody invited them into said conversation because…black widow…kiss of death.

She wondered how soon before she could excuse herself, go home, climb into bed and pull the covers up over her head.

She sipped her wine and glanced at Harry, found him watching her with a frown in his eyes. She didn't know how to answer the question there, so she merely shrugged. 'You'd have had more fun this evening if you'd surrendered me to Edith and her gang.'

'You're wrong. You and I have Very Important Things to discuss.'

He said the words as if they should have capitals. 'Oh?'

'The thing is…'

He leaned across the table towards her and it felt as if not just the table shrank but the entire room. It was possible that every eye in the room was on them, but in that brief moment she didn't care.

Which was also dangerous, but so damn freeing she couldn't help glorying in it. She reminded herself about the playboy thing.

'What *is* the thing?' she found herself asking.

Her pulse was *not* racing and her breath was *not* hitching.

'You and I need to make a deal. Wedding attendants have to stick together. It's the *rules*.'

She fought a smile. 'The rules, huh?'

'Exactly. Which means I hereby solemnly swear to save you from the great-aunts' table as long as you promise to save me from the scary ladies' table.'

She glanced in the direction he indicated and a laugh shot from her. A little too loudly, obviously, because it suddenly felt as if the entire room stared at her.

'Susie's cousins,' she said, trying to school her features. 'And I guess you could call them a little scary. But rumour has it there's not a scary ladies' table in all the land that holds any fear for you.'

He wagged a finger at her. 'Wrong answer. You haven't promised me yet.'

She choked back another laugh. 'Okay, okay, you have a deal.'

'Thank you!'

He sounded heartfelt.

'I could kiss you. Except I'm off kissing and romance and all of that nonsense.'

'Oh, ho! Another drink for the gentleman, please.' She seized a wine bottle and topped up his glass. 'Colour me intrigued. This is a story I have to hear.'

'It's not as interesting as it sounds.'

She couldn't work out if he was mock rueful or whether the regret was real. 'Why don't you let me be the judge of that?' It had to be more interesting than her life at the moment.

He sat back, gave a shrug. 'Well, for reasons…'

Ones he obviously didn't want to go into.

'I need to clean up my image. I have to channel less of the party boy and more of the clean-cut role model.'

She glanced at the scary ladies' table. 'So you're trying to stay away from temptation.'

He huffed out a curiously mirthless laugh. 'That's the problem: it's what everyone thinks—that I'm constantly on the prowl. Wherever I go, even if it's just a quiet dinner with friends, compromising pictures of me somehow get leaked to the press, as if it's a game. In reality they're not compromising. In reality it's usually just some girl who's had too much to drink throwing her arms around me, and her friends snapping a picture.'

Was he serious? But…that was awful!

His eyes narrowed. 'And experience tells me that the women on the table over there would find something like that a hoot, a great joke. And I'm tired of being the butt of everyone's jokes.'

'Oh, Harry.' Her chest burned. 'I'm sorry.'

'Not your fault.'

'Yeah, well, I could've been more sensitive rather than jumping to conclusions.'

'Conclusions fed by the press.'

She stared at him, wishing she could make him smile again. 'We shouldn't believe everything we read.'

'Yeah, well, I'm not saying I'm a saint either.'

It sounded like a warning. 'I never thought that for a moment.'

His gaze sharpened. 'You and I—' he gestured between them '—are on the same wavelength.'

She took in that square jaw, the white-blond hair and those ridiculously broad shoulders and a pulse started up inside her.

She pulled back. She had no intention of viewing Harry in *that* kind of light. But with his soulful brown eyes and wicked-as-sin grin, he was the kind of man who *oozed* sex appeal, and she'd be a fool to let her guard down around him. He might say he was trying to clean up his image but that could just be a line he was spinning. Or a promise he wasn't capable of keeping.

And she wasn't in the market for anything like that. 'What makes you think we're on the same wavelength?'

'You can't breathe a word of this to another soul.'

She wasn't breathing too much of anything to anyone at the moment so she crossed her heart.

'Before we came into the restaurant, Martin told me you were sad and asked me to cheer you up.'

She sat back, stung, though his words shouldn't have surprised her.

'But it took me less than half an hour to work out that you're not sad.'

He knew that? *How?* And how could she convince everyone else of that fact?

'You're not sad, but everyone else is.'

His words speared into all the sore places in her heart. It took all her strength not to lower her head to the table and close her eyes.

'So *I* don't need to cheer *you* up. What *we* need to do is find a way to cheer everyone else up or this wedding is going to be about as much fun as...'

'Balancing the books?' she offered. The thought of spending her life balancing books made her want to scream. Really loudly.

'There's a certain satisfaction in having balanced the books. No, this wedding is in danger of becoming a—'

He broke off. 'A wake?' she said softly.

He grimaced. 'Sorry.'

'Don't be daft. No apologies necessary.' She didn't want him walking on eggshells around her.

His gaze held hers and it felt as if he plumbed her very depths. And then he nodded and she let out a breath, realising he'd taken her words exactly as she'd meant them, that he'd accepted she wasn't some delicate flower in danger of breaking.

He sent a pointed glance at Susie and Martin and then hitched his head at the rest of the room. 'We need to do something to fix this.'

She'd been trying to, but her best efforts clearly weren't good enough. But with Harry's help…

Maybe he was right. Maybe they were on the same wavelength. She leaned towards him. 'I'd love to cheer everyone up, Harry. I'd love to make this a wedding Susie could look back on with pride, one not marred by grief.'

'Then we're on the same page.'

She chewed the inside of her cheek. 'Speaking of the wedding, do you know what they have planned? Something's afoot and—'

'Can I have a bit of shush?' Martin chose that moment to rise to his feet and tap his wine glass with his knife to get everyone's attention. 'Susie and I have a rather important announcement to make.'

CHAPTER TWO

ELLA SLUMPED AT the bar and glared into her diet cola, wishing it were something *much* stronger. She barely glanced at Harry when he slid onto the stool beside her. 'They're gone?'

'Every last one of them,' he said with a cheerfulness that set her teeth on edge.

Don't begrudge him his good mood. You should be sharing it, you ungrateful wretch.

She made herself straighten and send him a smile. 'Quiet at last.' She closed her eyes and pretended to relish it. Not that much pretence was necessary. 'How's the serenity?'

When she opened her eyes she saw her oblique reference to the iconic Australian film *The Castle* had made his lips lift.

Which, it had to be said, lifted her spirits a fraction too, so there was that.

She dragged her gaze away before it could become anything more. She didn't want him thinking she was in the market for anything like that. And if he wasn't looking for anything of that na-

ture either—and he hadn't said or done anything
to give her reason to think otherwise—she didn't
want to be lumped in with the scary ladies.

'I'll have what she's having,' he said when the
bartender came over.

'It's diet,' she warned.

'But not diet,' he added, before glancing back at
Ella. 'You look like you'd prefer something stronger.'

She pointed a finger at him. 'Perhaps we are
on the same wavelength after all.' Rather than
emerging light and teasing, though, an edge of bitterness laced her words, making her wince. 'But
you know... I need to get home in one piece, so
it's time to switch to the soft stuff.'

His nostrils flared fractionally. Harry really did
have the most classically handsome nose to go
with that classically handsome face. He had the
kind of face that a girl could enjoy staring at for
a very, *very* long time.

'Are you driving?'

The question was carefully asked, but she
sensed the disapproval behind it. 'Oh, Harry, that
wavelength thing just took a bit of a battering. Of
course I'm not driving. I'm always far too tempted
at these things to have one glass too many. Also,
driving from the southwest of the city to the north-
east on a Friday afternoon in peak-hour traffic is
not my idea of fun. It was quicker to take the train
and taxi it from the station.'

'Sorry, I should've realised.'

There was absolutely no reason he should've realised anything. Despite what he said, he didn't know her from Adam…or Eve.

'Oh!' She straightened. 'Were you hoping for a lift home?'

'Of course not.'

He said it too quickly and then she saw what this was and her chest clenched. 'You've been co-opted into Ella duty, haven't you?'

His grimace gave him away. For God's sake, she didn't need babysitting!

'I promised your dad I'd see you safely home.'

'I'm a grown woman.'

'I don't feel good about it either, but…'

She raised an eyebrow.

'I had the distinct impression it was either promise that, or they'd…'

'Babysit me?'

'Shepherd you back to the family home for the night. I thought maybe this was the lesser of two evils.'

He had a point.

One deliciously broad shoulder lifted. 'If it bugs you that much, I won't, though.'

She straightened. 'You mean that?'

'I'd hate not keeping my word to your dad, but I'm not into forcing my company onto women who don't want it.'

She believed him. Harry Gillespie might have

the face—and body, don't forget the body—of a God, but he didn't have an ego that went with it.

'That said, I'd like to see you home, Ella. But not on the train. Let me spring for a taxi. Everyone knows I'm loaded, and what's the point in being wealthy if you can't make things comfortable for yourself and your friends?'

Were they friends? She took a deliberate sip of her cola, before setting her glass down. 'I won't be inviting you inside once we get there.'

'Even if you did,' he said gently, 'I'd refuse your very kind invitation.'

His words shouldn't sting. They'd been uttered far more graciously than hers. It made no sense. The lack of sense, however, didn't temper the sting.

'I do have an ulterior motive, though. I want the skinny on everything and everyone. So you might as well ride in comfort while I pump you for information.'

She laughed, but she sensed he wasn't joking.

'And it means we can both have that one last drink we're dying for rather than this—' he flicked a finger at his glass '—lolly water.'

Did he think another drink would get her rolling drunk? She hadn't drunk anywhere near as much as everyone thought she had. This would be her third glass of wine for the entire evening. Oh, different family members had poured many more for her, but she'd left those glasses in various out of the way places and had sipped water instead.

His lips twitched. 'I'm not trying to get you drunk so I can take advantage of you.'

Her face suddenly burned. 'I never thought any such thing.'

'Liar.' But he grinned as he said it.

'Well, not in the way you think,' she admitted. 'I meant in the "alcohol is a truth serum" kind of way. Another glass of wine isn't going to get me drunk. It'll put me over the limit for driving, it'll give me a pleasant buzz, but it won't have me throwing caution to the winds, dancing on the tables, and divulging all of my deep dark secrets... or anyone else's.'

'I don't want secrets.' He frowned. 'At least I don't think I do.'

'What do you want, then?'

'I'll have another of those,' he said to the barman, pointing to the tap of craft beer she'd ordered for him earlier, and then raised an eyebrow at her. 'Sémillon?'

Whether it was wise or not, she nodded.

She didn't know if she ought to be on her guard around Harry or to trust her instincts and take him at face value. One thing was in his favour—he was Martin's best friend. While Martin might not be able to look her in the eye at the moment, he was still a good guy. Her dad trusted him enough to ask him to see her home. The family were all driving her mad at the moment, but if anything about Harry had rung alarm bells for them, they'd all be sitting here playing guard dog.

She raised her glass in salute and took a sip before saying, 'Grill away. What do you want to know?'

He gazed into his glass, lips pursed.

He had nice lips. They seemed to be forever on the verge of spilling laughter and—

She jolted back to earth. Swallowing, she spread her hands. 'You have to give me something to work with here, Harry.'

He turned more fully towards her. 'I don't think the two of us should tiptoe around each other. Agreed?'

Suited her just fine. She was tired of everyone walking on eggshells. 'Agreed, especially if we're to save this wedding.' He looked a little too serious, though, so she added, 'Besides, there's the wavelength thing to consider. If we're so attuned to each other, you'll know when I'm lying, right? So it'd be pointless.'

The thought made her frown. While she'd been turning the wavelength thing into a joke, making light of it, a ribbon of truth threaded beneath it. In some odd way, she did feel connected to Harry. It wasn't the most comfortable thought she'd had all evening.

She huffed out the smallest of laughs. It wasn't

the most uncomfortable one either, though, so there was that.

He spread his arms. 'See? Friends at first sight.'

She made herself laugh, made that laugh sound as if she thought him ridiculous. But that didn't stop her heart from thump-thumping or prevent warmth from curling in the pit of her stomach.

'So no faffing about or beating around the bush,' he ordered. 'Our policy is to be upfront and honest. We've a lot of work to do.'

'Agreed.' They shook on it.

'So first of all, I want to know why you hate the thought of an all-expenses-paid week in a luxury resort in Malaysia.'

Ah.

He leaned in closer. She had no idea what aftershave he wore, but she caught hints of leather and smoke, amber and resin. She wondered if they sold that scent in candles. If they did she was buying ten of them first thing tomorrow.

'You hated the idea so much you weren't able to convince a single solitary person in the room otherwise, even though you said all the right things and made all the right noises.'

Guilt bit at her. 'Was it really that obvious? You sure that's not the wavelength thing talking?'

'Not the wavelength thing. *Very* obvious.'

She swore.

'What's the story?'

'It's not Malaysia. I've nothing whatsoever

against Malaysia. The resort sounds fantastic. And even though I shouldn't take too much time off work at the moment...' Except she could now, couldn't she? If she was going to turn her back on it all and return to the family business.

A howl started up at the centre of her.

'Then what is it?'

His eyes didn't leave her face, and he asked the question so gently it took all her strength not to drop her head to the bar and weep. 'It's the week they've chosen.'

Susie and Martin's wedding would now take place in one month's time—on a gorgeous Malaysian beach—and the bride's and groom's families were paying for everyone present at the restaurant this evening to attend. In theory it sounded like dream-come-true stuff. In reality...

'A month is long enough for us to work our magic, if that's what you're worried about,' he assured her. 'We can turn this thing around and make it the funnest damn wedding that ever was.'

She didn't want to make it the funnest damn wedding ever. She wanted to rant and rail and tell them all she was sick to death of the way they were trying to control her. She wanted to throw the bridesmaid towel in and tell Susie to find someone else for the job.

She couldn't of course. That would be over-reacting. She pulled in a breath to the count of six, released it again just as slowly. 'In one month's time, on that exact week, I'm supposed to be showcasing my business at a fashion expo. It was a major step in getting my name and brand out there. I've been working on this for more than six months.'

'You're a fashion designer?'

'Of sorts. This is an alternative fashion expo, showcasing sustainable garments and practices. Sustainable sewing is gaining mainstream traction and—' she shrugged '—it's something I feel passionate about. So while I do some designing and take the odd commission—' because people were prepared to pay an insane amount of money for what they considered a couture one-off item '—I'm building towards the launch of my own online sewing school.'

Except none of that mattered now if she planned to return to the family business, did it?

He leaned in closer as if utterly intrigued. 'So you're a seamstress, fashion designer, sewing teacher and environmental crusader?'

She sent him a weak smile. 'Just call me Wonder Woman.'

'You made this?' He handed her off her stool and made her pirouette.

'Both skirt and blouse are thrift-store refashions.'

'They're amazing. You look amazing.'

There was a *but* behind his words. She slid back onto her stool. 'But?'

He grimaced.

'You were the one who said we needed to be upfront and honest,' she pointed out.

'It's just…the colours aren't very cheerful.'

She glanced down and blinked. He was right. She had a wardrobe full of colourful clothes, and yet she couldn't remember the last time she'd worn any of them. Had she been channelling her gloom and resentment into her clothing choices? Because the family was making her feel *less* at the moment? Less capable. Less than she was. Less *everything*.

'Okay, observation noted and taken on board.' That was definitely something she could work on.

'You're not offended?'

'Nope.' She sipped her wine.

'I didn't mean I don't like the outfit. It's fabulous. You look great in it.'

'Relax, Harry, I'm not offended.' She gestured at her outfit. 'And as you can see, I'm good at what I do.' Her lips twisted. 'I just need to get the word out there.'

'Does Susie know about the fashion expo? Because—'

'She knows.'

She hadn't challenged Susie about it tonight because… She swallowed. Because she hadn't been honest with Susie in recent times, and if she started now it might lead to questions. An ugly ball of darkness twisted in her stomach. Questions she didn't want to answer.

Still, how could Susie do this to her? It was all she could do to stop her hands from clenching. It'd serve her right if Ella told her to find a new bridesmaid. The next moment, though, her shoulders slumped. She didn't mean it. If she did that it'd break Susie's heart, and while Ella might be angry enough to scream she wouldn't hurt Susie for the world. She knew the family would've railroaded her en masse to choose this particular date for the wedding. Susie wouldn't have been able to withstand them.

Dark blond brows lowered over throbbing brown eyes. Ella shrugged. 'They all know.'

His frown deepened. 'What am I missing? If everyone knows about the expo, knows how important it is to you, then why…?'

'Because they don't support what I'm doing. They don't believe me when I tell them that running my own online sewing school is the dream of my heart and what I want to do with my life. They think it's a reckless decision I've made in response to James's death.'

'But it's not.'

It wasn't a question but a statement. It felt like a recognition—that he saw what it meant to her and implicitly trusted in that. 'The problem is, I hadn't told anyone about it before James died.'

He blinked. 'Not even James?'

'Oh, no, James knew.' They'd been fighting about it. He'd hated the idea as much as everyone else appeared to. Her heart squeezed in her chest. The knowledge that his final days would've been happier if she'd never raised the topic with him could still make her wake up in a cold sweat in the middle of the night.

'So—' he tapped a finger against his half-empty glass '—it feels as if it's come out of the blue for them.'

'More like a bomb that's exploded.'

His frown deepened. It took an effort not to reach up and smooth out the lines on his forehead.

And maybe she ought to stop drinking right about now.

'What were you doing prior to being a seamstress extraordinaire? What do they think could possibly top that?'

On second thoughts… She gulped her Sémillon. 'I was working in the family business—business consultancy and management.'

His jaw dropped. And then he swore. 'Ella, you're in a right pickle, aren't you? Because they're not going to think anything can top that.'

Bingo. 'A rock and a hard place,' she agreed.

They sipped their drinks and were silent for a bit. 'This is deliberate sabotage against your business.'

'That's not how they'd phrase it. They'd say they were saving me from myself.'

'It's crossing a line and it's not fair.'

'Don't I know it. And if I'm not careful I'm going to explode soon, Harry.' She'd say things she shouldn't. She'd say things she'd regret. She'd say things she could never take back, and they'd been hurt enough. 'I don't want that to happen. I know they're hurting—that this is all tied up in their grief for James.' She stared down at her hands. 'I've started to think I should just keep the peace and return to the family business.'

'You can't do that!'

It was nice of him to sound so outraged on her behalf, but—

'Ella, you *can't* do that.' He rested a warm hand on her forearm and squeezed gently until she met his gaze. 'You'll regret it forever. Worse, you'll resent them for it. It might look like a short-term quick fix, but in the long run...' He shook his head. 'Don't do this to yourself.'

Your dreams are just as important as everyone else's.

Maybe they were. Maybe they weren't. But, God, she was *so tired*.

'I honestly think we can turn things around and have everyone enjoying the upcoming celebrations. I think we can make this a wedding that will be remembered for all the right reasons.'

She stared. 'You're not just saying that?'

He pressed a hand to his heart. 'I believe we can do it.'

His expression was all fierce focus, and beneath it she saw the determination that had won him several world championships.

He leant down until they were eye to eye. 'I know you're feeling overwhelmed, you've had to deal with all of this on your own for far too long, but you have help now.'

She had help... Some unknown weight lifted off her shoulders. 'I could kiss you for saying that. Except, you know, you're off kissing. And so am I.' It seemed prudent to add that last bit.

He grinned. 'See? You're already entering into the spirit.'

She was?

'We just need to find a way, or ways, to stop them worrying about you. Once we show them it's okay to laugh around you again, not only will we be able to rescue the wedding, but we might even prove to them that you're in charge of your own destiny—that your sewing school is an excellent plan.'

Her heart thumped all the way up into her throat. 'I want to believe that so badly.' She wanted to believe her family could be happy again. She wanted to believe that she didn't have to sacrifice her dream.

'Then believe it. And don't make any drastic decisions about your business until after the wedding. Deal?'

A month? It didn't seem like too much to ask.

If, at the end of that time, the family were still unhappy with her choices… She swallowed. Well, she could give her dream up then. In the meantime she could hold it close. She nodded. 'Deal.'

Damn! No wonder Ella's discontent at Martin and Susie's wedding plans had been so transparent. Her entire family as well as Susie's—and it appeared they were pretty much one and the same—were conspiring against her. In her shoes he'd—

What? an inner voice mocked. *Rebel?*

He rolled his shoulders. Maybe not, but he'd be chafing in the same way Ella chafed, while trying to be as careful with everyone's feelings as she was trying to be.

He scratched both hands back through his hair. She'd had a lot to deal with over the last eighteen months. She deserved a break.

And Martin and Susie deserved a great wedding.

He bumped shoulders with her. 'Before we start brainstorming ways to cheer everyone up, there's an issue we need to clear up first.'

She raised one finely shaped eyebrow. *Nice* eyebrow. Nice eyes—*so* blue. Actually, she had a nice face. *Really* nice and—

Focus, Harrison.

He shook himself. 'Right, why not go to the expo instead of attending the wedding?'

She grabbed hold of the bar as if she were in danger of falling, her mouth opening and closing. 'Harry, Susie is practically my *sister*. I can't *not* go to her wedding. That'd be—' She broke off and shook her head. 'That's not even remotely an option.'

'Sorry, I just thought…' He grimaced. 'I was speaking with my practical business hat on. My family aren't like yours and Susie's.' *Obviously.* He could feel his lips twist, even though he tried to stop them. 'In my family, business always comes first.'

Blue eyes frowned into his. 'I know I'm losing patience with them and feeling resentful. But family comes first Harry. *Always.*'

How different would his family have been if—? *Don't even go there.*

He slapped a hand to the bar. 'Okay, then we need to work out how to get your business represented at that expo. You must have an employee you trust enough to act as your representative.'

Amusement turned her eyes even bluer. 'Oh, listen to you, world champion skier and super-successful businessman.'

'Former world champion,' he corrected.

'No wonder you've been so successful with a won't-say-die attitude like that.'

He stared. And then he swallowed. She'd focussed on his success, rather than his wealth. That was…

'What?'

'Nothing. I just…' He trailed off with a shrug.

'You're a problem solver. I get that. But I'm a one-woman band, Harry. I don't have any employees, trusted or otherwise. Sew Sensational currently comprises…me.'

He felt the size of a pea. Not everyone had the money he had. What an entitled jerk she must think him.

'I only struck out on my own six months ago. Until I start turning a decent profit, I'm going to remain a one-woman band.'

He read between the lines. James had died eighteen months ago. She'd given herself over to the family business for the twelve months following his death.

Because she'd been too grief-stricken to think straight?

Or because she hadn't wanted to create too much upheaval in her family's life all at once?

She'd said the family business was business consulting and management. 'You have a business degree?'

She nodded.

'It's not like you've gone into this venture of yours blind or with blinkers on, then.'

'Absolutely not.' She twirled her glass around slowly, staring at the golden liquid inside. 'I'm fully versed in the traps that lie in wait for the unwary. I've spent over a year building a platform on YouTube, establishing a clientele, and running sewing classes at the local community college. I have a stall at the local monthly markets. I've focussed hard on building a solid base, and I make enough money to pay the bills from the activities I now engage in. The expo was supposed to launch the second phase of operations. While it's only a small boutique-style event, it's been garnering interest in all of the right circles. To have my sewing school's name linked to it, get it endorsed by the right people…'

She trailed off, her shoulders drooping. He was shocked at how much he wanted to make her smile again.

'If it went well, it was going to provide me with the right credentials to launch the school with the appropriate fanfare.'

And he could see that her vision for the sewing school was the passion that powered all the rest.

He clapped his hands. 'Right, then. What we need to do is find you someone who can represent you at the expo and—'

'No.'

No? What did she mean, *no*?

'This is my problem, Harry, not yours. I don't want you offering to invest in my business or to lend me a trusted employee or three of your own or…anything. It's my company and if I'm going to keep going I need to find my own solutions.'

He really wanted to help. But her need to feel

in control of at least one aspect of her life was far more important than anything he might want. Very reluctantly he raised his hands. 'Okay, but I hope you'll let me know if there's anything I can do.'

She frowned, as if his sincerity surprised her.

'Look, I'm considered a successful business-man.'

She huffed out a laugh. 'You're stating the obvious now.'

'But I didn't start from nothing. Not like you. I inherited a trust fund and had backers.'

His company dealt in adventure ski holidays. They helicoptered their clientele to some of the most remote ski fields in the world, where they stayed in chateaus whose luxury was unsurpassed. He'd spared no expense on any of it. The very rich were prepared to spend an exorbitant amount of money for the very best. Especially when it was endorsed by a former alpine ski champion.

Her soft laugh warmed him from the inside out. 'Nobody handed you those world titles on a silver platter. You worked hard for them all on your own.'

'That's not exactly true. I had a team surrounding me—coaches, managers, physios. Plus,' he added when she opened her mouth to argue, 'my parents were wealthy enough to indulge the ski lessons and clinics I wanted. I was fortunate.'

'And unnecessarily humble.'

She reached out and clasped his forearm. 'I appreciate the offer, I really do.' She dropped her hand again almost immediately, but her touch sent a flicker of heat licking along his veins. His pulse pounded and his heart thudded. The curve of her lips when she—

No! He would *not* develop an inconvenient attraction to this woman. His stomach churned. She was exactly the kind of woman he avoided. Women like Ella got hurt by men like him. And it was clear she'd been through enough in the last eighteen months.

Ella stared into her nearly empty glass with pursed lips, completely oblivious to his turmoil. Which was good. Perfect, in fact. He didn't want her aware.

He just needed to master the wilful compulsion that now gripped him to shake her out of her complacency and force her to see him as a man. Talk about self-destructive impulses! He ground his back molars together, reminded himself of all the reasons it was important to win the confidence of the trustees of the Bright Directions charity, reminded himself that he wasn't his father!

Seizing his beer, he drained it before slamming it back to the bar. 'Ready to hit the road?'

She blinked. 'I...yeah, sure.'

If his abruptness startled her, she was far too polite to say so.

But as the taxi wove its way from the harbour

towards the address she'd given the driver, the silence in the cab grew oppressive.

'Look, Harry, I'm sorry if I offended you.'

The air was scented with peaches—probably her shampoo or body wash—and it was oddly alluring. He tried to not breathe in too deeply. 'Offended me?'

'By not accepting your offer of help.'

'I'm not offended!'

Those finely shaped brows rose. He ignored the desire to reach out and trace a finger across one delicate arc. 'Two things. The first is that I flew into Australia yesterday from Switzerland and jet lag has started to kick in. So my responses are probably off kilter.' He sure as hell felt off kilter.

'Uh-huh.' She didn't sound convinced.

'And two, I'm outraged on your behalf at this stunt The Family have pulled on you.'

Her lips twitched. 'The family capitalised?'

'If the shoe fits,' he murmured.

She pushed a stray curl back behind her ear. 'Okay, so missing the expo is a setback, but if I'm going to forge ahead with Sew Sensational...'

She *had* to. She couldn't give up her dream.

One slim shoulder lifted. 'Then I can't let things like this derail me. So please, Harry, forget about the expo. At the moment we have bigger fish to fry. We need to focus on the wedding.'

'The fish we have to fry are pretty big,' he agreed. The task before them suddenly felt gargantuan. And the stakes were high. But if they could pull this off, then maybe Ella wouldn't abandon her dream. He couldn't explain why it mattered so much. Only that it did.

He stifled a yawn and she smiled. For one heart-jerking moment he thought she meant to pat his arm, but she lowered her hand back to her lap before it had a chance to reach him. He couldn't believe how much he wanted to drag her into his arms and kiss her. He clenched his hands. He really needed a good night's sleep.

'However, we don't have to come up with a plan right now,' she said. 'Why don't you rest for a while—get some shut-eye while you can?'

There wasn't a hope in hell he'd get a moment's sleep sitting this close to her, but he could pretend. And pretending was definitely the wisest course of action at the moment. 'Promise you'll wake me when we get to your place?'

'I promise.'

He closed his eyes and although he'd thought he'd continue to prickle and burn, her undemanding presence and the scent of peaches were oddly soothing. He didn't fall asleep, but to simply be quiet and have a chance to allow his body to adjust to the time zone felt like a gift.

He immediately opened his eyes, though, when the taxi stopped. He didn't want her shaking him awake. He didn't want her touching him at all.

Not now he'd lulled the slathering beast inside him into a semblance of slumber.

She gestured out of the window. 'This is me.'

He stared and then he straightened. 'You live in a warehouse?' That was cool. Seriously cool.

She blinked, at whatever she saw in his face. And then smiled. Oh, God. *Don't focus on those lips.* 'These are my business premises. I live in the flat above. I know it's not particularly grand, but—' she frowned, turning back to stare at it '—it's not just a glorified garage either.'

He stiffened. 'Who called it that? I'll bop them on the nose.'

She raised one of those ridiculously beautiful eyebrows and he let out a slow breath. Her family. That was who. The people who should be supporting her dreams. Didn't she have anyone to share the excitement of all this with?

'These digs are cool, Ella. Seriously cool. I'd love to see inside.' He jerked back. 'But not tonight! That's not what I meant.' He didn't want her thinking he was a sleaze. 'I just meant in daylight hours when I could appreciate it properly and—'

He broke off with a groan, but she just laughed. 'Relax, I know what you meant.' She bit her lip. 'If you're serious…'

'I'm serious.' He was definitely serious.

'Do you have a busy weekend ahead of you?'

'Nope.'

'Then why don't you come to lunch on Sunday?

Midday-ish? And I'll give you the grand tour. And maybe we can throw around a few ideas for how to pep everyone up and give Susie and Martin the wedding of the year.'

'I'll bring a bottle of wine and my imagination.'

'Perfect. It's a date.' She'd started to turn away to open her door, but froze before glancing back over her shoulder. 'I didn't mean *date* date. It was just a turn of phrase, a figure of speech, not—'

'Relax, Ella, I know what you meant.' He got the message loud and clear.

'No, no, stay there,' she said when he made to get out of the taxi to walk her to her door. 'Jet lag, remember. There's a sensor light that'll come on. Just wait until I get inside and you'll have performed your duty admirably.'

He couldn't kiss her. This wasn't a date. 'Goodnight, Ella.'

'Night, Harry, sleep tight.'

And then she was gone, but heat continued to thread its way through his veins with an insidious viciousness that made him scowl as the taxi turned around and took him back towards the city centre.

CHAPTER THREE

ELLA HEARD A car draw up outside, probably her-
alding Harry's arrival, but she forced herself to
remain at her sewing machine, rather than rushing to the door to check. She'd already spent far
too long today—and yesterday—thinking about
Martin's best man.

And the last thing she needed was to start ob-
sessing over some guy. Lord, talk about a glutton
for punishment!

Besides, it'd only be a displacement activity and
she couldn't afford one of those. Not if she planned
to cling to her sewing-school dream. Harry's
words on Friday night had given her hope. They'd
reinvigorated the fire in her belly.

To drive her point home, she concentrated extra
hard on sewing her seam utterly, perfectly and di-
vinely straight. When she was done, and only after
she'd snipped the thread, did she answer the prick-
ling at the back of her neck and turn her head.

Harry stood in the open doorway, and the
breath hitched in the back of her throat. The

sunlight pouring in behind him left his face in shadow, but the lean, broad height of him was backlit, showcasing the muscular power of a body in its physical prime.

Dear God. She'd known on some level on Friday night that he was fit and athletic—*hello, former world champion*—but she'd been too dazzled by his grin and easy manner—and the fact he hadn't known James—to pay attention to much else.

She had to swallow before she could speak. 'Harry, it's nice to see you again. Come on in.'

When he strode into the large room, the overhead lighting revealed that chiselled jaw, sculpted cheekbones and…dear God, *that grin*…and she immediately forgave herself for not noticing anything else on Friday night. She'd thought perhaps she'd exaggerated his, uh…assets because she'd been so desperate for a little respite from her family.

But, no, the man was a hundred and ten per cent pure male perfection.

'You're working?'

His words snapped her back. 'I'm always tinkering.' She leapt up to take the bottle of wine he carried. 'The thing about my work is that it never feels like work.' She glanced at the bottle's label, and something warm slid beneath her guard. He'd brought a Sémillon. He'd remembered what she liked to drink?

A hot guy was a temptation she could resist. But a hot, *considerate* guy…?

Stop it. Obviously she had every intention of resisting one of those too, but… It struck her then that she liked Harry. As a person. He was a good guy.

'Is there something wrong with the wine?'

She started. 'No! It's great. I…you remembered what I was drinking the other night.'

He looked suddenly discomfited, as if worried she'd read too much into it.

Oh, for heaven's sake, Ella, it's just a bottle of wine.

'It's very thoughtful of you, and puts us on a par, because I remembered you drank beer and I got some in specially,' she tossed over her shoulder as she moved towards the kitchen.

He immediately relaxed. 'See? I keep telling you we're on the same wavelength.'

The kitchen was situated to one side of the main doors, separated from the rest of the room by a large counter with glass sliders. There wasn't enough room in the kitchen for a table but she'd set a table on the workshop side of the counter the very first day she'd moved in.

She stowed the wine in the fridge. Harry trailed along behind her. 'Your kitchen and bathroom are downstairs?'

'The upstairs flat has its own kitchen and bathroom, but I find myself eating down here more often than not.'

'Because you're working so much?'

There was no censure in his voice, as there would be in her mother's if she'd asked the same question. 'Well, it's true that you can whip up a seam or two while something's simmering on the stovetop or heating in the oven, but more often than not in the evenings I just like to play around with an idea or two and...fiddle for the hell of it.'

His lips twitched. 'Which you don't consider work.'

Her lips twitched too. 'Of course not! It's play. And as there's far more room down here than up-stairs...'

'It's a no-brainer.'

But he raised an eyebrow and she found herself laughing. 'Okay. If you want the pure, unadulter-ated truth—' she gestured at her workshop '—I know it's not exactly what one would call pretty, but...' She tried to put the feeling into words. 'It makes my heart sing. It makes me ridiculously happy to look at it and realise it's mine—my own little kingdom. So I eat down here more often than not because in those brief moments of downtime I get to relish that feeling.'

She hadn't tried to articulate that sentiment to anyone before. It surprised her how easily she'd been able to express it to Harry now. Brown eyes the colour of a deep smoky topaz turned to her, an arrested expression in their depths, and an itch started up between her collarbones. She shrugged—a stilted movement that made her feel suddenly graceless. 'I don't know. Maybe that sounds a little pathetic and sad, but—'

'*No!* Hell, Ella, you're living your dream, making that dream a reality. You should be milking every drop of joy from it that you can. Some people go through their whole lives never feeling this way. It's not sad and it's not pathetic. It's glorious and empowering. And it's all yours.'

Her eyes prickled and she had to blink hard. She should've known he'd understand. The man was a former world champion. He'd obviously had a dream once too. Hers seemed so much smaller in comparison.

'Please tell me you're not giving this up without a fight.'

Her dream might not be huge and lofty, but it didn't make it any less worthy. She pushed her shoulders back. 'I'll fight. I know the family can't see it, but I'd be miserable if I had to go back to business consultancy. If I can make a success of my online sewing school…' Her heart pounded. 'Eventually they'll start to worry less.' Wouldn't they?

'Especially once they realise how happy you are.'

Therein lay the rub. It was hard to be happy

around them when it felt as if they were continually waiting for her to crash and burn.

A knock sounded on the door. 'Harrison? Hello?'

Harry shot out of the kitchen. 'Lily? What's up?'

'You're lucky I love you. You dropped your phone in the car. I jumped out of my skin when it rang. I thought you'd probably need it.'

The woman's words made Ella blink.

'And now I'm going to be late so—'

She broke off when she saw Ella.

He glanced at Ella and gestured. 'This is my little sister, Lily.'

Sister? She refused to acknowledge the relief rippling through her. It was entirely unworthy of her.

'And, Lil, this is—'

'Sew Sensational's Ella! *Oh, my God!*' She leapt forward to pump Ella's hand. 'I subscribe to your YouTube channel. I think you're amazing.'

Harry's brow pleated. 'You mentioned you had a YouTube channel.'

Ella tried to contain a grin. She had a fan? A real bona fide fan?'

Lily glanced around at the workshop, hands clasped beneath her chin. 'And this is where the magic happens?'

Magic? Oh, had she ever had a nicer compliment? 'It is. Do you sew, Lily?'

A shadow fell across the other woman's face. 'No, but…'

She heard that 'but' a lot—*but* I want to…*but* I wish I could…*but* I don't know where to start. There were endless variations.

'God, this room! It…'

'It what?' Harry demanded, a frown lurking in his eyes.

Lily swung back. 'It reminds me of my mother.'

Harry froze.

'She had a sewing room.' She sent Ella a smile. 'Obviously not on this scale. She was going to teach me, but…'

She heard a lot of those 'buts' too. And everyone knew how successful Harry's mother was. Claudia King was CEO of the mining dynasty King Holdings. Had she become too busy to teach her daughter to sew?'

'Do you run sewing classes? Please say yes.'

Ella did her best to project a professional image, but inside a huge smile stretched through her. 'I'm in the process of setting up an online sewing school. I'm hoping to take it live in the next few months.'

'Oh, that's perfect.' Lily clapped her hands and bounced. 'Absolutely perfect.' Her gaze continued to rove hungrily around the room, and her eyes widened when they landed on Susie's wedding dress on the mannequin. She pointed. 'That's breathtaking.'

'It's for a beach wedding so it's a little less formal than a lot of wedding gowns. For my friend Susie…' She gestured at Harry and herself. 'The wedding we're best man and bridesmaid for.'

Lily reached across and gripped Ella's hand. 'You and I really need to talk.'

She blinked. 'I… Okay.'

'Why?' Harry barked, staring from Lily to the wedding dress and back again. He pointed. 'You are not…'

It sounded like an order rather than a question, but Lily merely rolled her eyes and ignored him. 'Would you consider giving one-on-one lessons?' she asked Ella.

'I…' She hadn't thought about it.

Lily's phone pinged and she grimaced. 'I have to go, but—' She transferred her grip to Harry's arm. 'You have to bring Ella to dinner some time soon. Promise?'

He glanced at Ella and raised an eyebrow. She nodded. Dinner with a fan? Yes, please! That could be the boost her flagging spirits needed.

'Okay, okay, I'll bring her to dinner. Now stop manhandling her, Lil, and get out of here. And drive safe!'

'It was so nice to meet you,' she said with a wave at Ella. 'Wait until I tell Viggo.'

'Her boyfriend,' Harry murmured as Lily shot out of the door.

Then he turned to her more fully. 'What magic

have you woven to captivate my little sister so completely?'

She shrugged. 'I…'

He frowned. 'What do you think she meant?' He gestured towards Susie's wedding dress.

'Are she and Viggo serious?'

'No!'

He glared, and she did what she could to choke back a laugh.

His glare became a scowl. 'What?'

'You're hilarious, you know that? All overprotective, bristling big brother,' she teased.

He grimaced but humour lightened his eyes. 'Old habits.' And then he frowned. 'I had no idea she wanted to sew.'

'Your mother never had the time to teach her?'

He gazed at her blankly for a moment, and then his face cleared. 'She was talking about her mother, not mine. Lily and I aren't really siblings, we're first cousins. Her parents died in a car accident when she was six and she came to live with us. Her father and my mother were siblings. I've always told her, though, that she's my little sister.'

Oh, that was nice. See? He really was a good guy.

'Tell me about your YouTube channel.'

'It's called Sew Sensational—spelled S-E-W— and I film sewing tips and tricks, give mini tutorials.'

He rubbed a hand across his jaw. 'You're obviously good. Lil's a damn fine judge of these things.'

She feigned surprise. 'You doubted it?'

That made him laugh. 'Not for a moment.' He glanced at Susie's wedding dress. 'You're making Susie's dress?'

'Susie's and mine. And the mums' outfits as well.'

He opened his mouth, closed it and then shook himself. 'Let me get this straight. Your family don't believe in your sewing business, yet they still want you to make their outfits for the wedding? That doesn't make sense.'

'They know I'm a good seamstress. They just don't think there's any money to be made in running an online sewing school,' she corrected. 'They consider sewing a hobby, not a business opportunity. They think it safer and smarter of me to remain in the family business.'

He was silent for a moment, but when he glanced up his gaze had sharpened. 'They want to keep you close because James is no longer here.'

That old heaviness descended on her. 'Do you think it's ungrateful of me to—?'

'No! What they're doing is unfair and selfish. Understandable because of their grief,' he added before she could defend them. 'But it'd be a grave mistake to submit to it, Ella.'

His words helped lift some of her heaviness.

He shook himself and grinned, and suddenly

there was no heaviness at all. 'Is lunch in danger of spoiling—it smells great, by the way—or do you have the time to give me the grand tour first?'

She gestured at her workshop. 'Well…this is it.'

'Nonsense. I want you to show me everything from go to whoa.'

She tried to slow the swirling excitement that had taken up residence in the pit of her stomach. Was he serious? Was he interested or just humouring her?

'Take me through the process if you were making a… I don't know—a dress.'

And in that moment she didn't care if he was truly interested or not. It was just exciting to share all of this with someone willing to listen. Nobody had shown this level of interest in what she was trying to do. *No one.*

She had a feeling it could become addictive.

Well, don't let it go to your head. And don't go overboard.

Two walls of the workshop were set up with her sewing machines and overlockers, while a series of built-in cupboards made up the third. In the centre of the room was her cutting table. She started by showing him her fabric stash, where he fingered some of the material and chuckled at some of her prints—particularly the ones with a sewing theme. When they moved to her drafting and cutting table, he inspected her various rulers and gauges, before she took him across to her sewing machines—six in total—and her two overlockers.

He gestured at the ironing board she had set up, a question in his eyes.

'It's good practice to press as you go.' And then she opened the doors beneath the drafting table.

He let out a breath. 'You have thread in every shade known to man. They look amazing. It makes you want to reach out and touch them.'

She felt the same way. Walking around, she opened a drawer on the other side. He followed to gaze at her neatly ordered rows of ribbons, buttons, lace trims, zippers, bias binding and cording. 'I don't even know what most of those things are called.'

'Notions.'

He opened the drawer nearest and pulled out an object, lifted it towards her in question.

'That's a tailor's ham. It helps press darts and contoured fabric patterns.'

'I don't even know what half of the words you're using mean. It's like a foreign language.'

And she could see that he wanted to understand it. That he liked to know how things worked.

'I do, however, know what these are.' He picked up her favourite pair of fabric shears. He hefted them from one hand to the other. 'They're heavy. You use these?'

'Every day. And don't even think about it,' she added when he went to cut through a piece of nearby scrap pattern paper. 'Nothing touches those hallowed blades except fabric.' She plucked a piece of cotton sateen from her offcuts bin and tossed it to him.

He cut along the sateen's length and a strange expression lit his face. 'God, that feels satisfying.'

She knew exactly what he meant.

'Oh, my God.' He set the shears down and raced across to the far corner. 'Now, this looks like fun.'

She laughed and stroked a finger across the casing of the sewing machine, its innards spread across the table. 'I service my own machines.'

His head whipped around. 'No way.' He stared at the assorted pieces. 'No wonder you've impressed Lil so much. You can do it all.'

He straightened, stuck his hands in his back pockets. 'You wouldn't let me help you put this back together by any chance, would you?'

She stifled a smile.

'It's just...this is an Aladdin's cave. I loved building stuff when I was a kid. Pulling a sewing machine apart, giving it a grease and oil change, and putting it back together could be fun.'

She stared at him for a moment. 'You can't help on this one because it requires a rather complicated repair and I'm waiting on a part, but...'

He leaned towards her. 'Yes?'

'Two of my machines are due for a service, so, if you're serious, after lunch we can take a machine each and I'll walk you through it.'

'You just became my new favourite person!'

She laughed, and went to tell him he was a cheap date, but choked the words back. This wasn't a date.

'And I want to know what you were working on when I arrived. You looked totally engrossed.'

Yeah, totally engrossed in trying not to look totally engrossed with him. But that reminded her...

'Not only am I making Susie's wedding dress, but I'm making the waistcoats for the groom and best man.'

'Martin and me?'

'I've Martin's measurements already, but do you mind if I grab yours now?' She seized her tape measure and a nearby pad and pencil. 'It should only take a sec.'

'Sure.'

'I was making a *toile*—a mock-up—of Martin's waistcoat when you arrived. I'll have him to try it on, so I can make any final adjustments to it before making the real thing.'

'Makes sense.'

She moved behind him and stretched the tape measure from shoulder to shoulder. A spasm convulsed through her the instant she touched him. The heat of him beat at her through his long-sleeved tee and crept beneath her skin. Heat and need and want flooded every atom of her body... And she didn't know what to do with any of it.

* * *

The moment Ella's fingers brushed his shoulders, air hissed from Harry's lungs. It was the lightest of touches, but, light or not, Ella's touch seared a path to his very bones and heat began to bubble in his veins. He gritted his teeth and silently started to recite the seven times table. The woman was simply doing her job, for God's sake.

Seven times four is twenty-eight. Seven times five is—

Her fingers moved from measuring the breadth of his shoulders to measuring shoulder to waist. Everything in between started to prickle and itch, while other parts—lower and higher—like his groin and his jaw, clenched.

He could hear the scratch of her pencil as she jotted the measurements down.

She moved in front of him, not meeting his eye.

Why would she meet your eye? She's not measuring your eyes. She's a professional. You're not a body to her but a series of measurements.

That last thought bolstered neither his strength nor his mood.

'Arms out,' she instructed, demonstrating.

He did as she asked, gritted his teeth as she measured him from armpit to waist. It drew her in closer and the scent of peaches rose up all around him. In that moment he'd give anything to sink his teeth into a sun-warmed peach. It wasn't the season for them, but maybe he could—

Stop! Fixating on peaches wasn't helping.

Seven times six is forty-two. Seven times seven—

She slipped the tape measure around his chest and… His nipples hardened. He bit back a groan. It was July. Winter in the southern hemisphere. Cold. The cold made nipples pebble. No big deal.

But the sun shone brightly outside and it was a mild nineteen degrees, not a frigid minus five on some alpine ski slope.

She moved away and he let out a breath, lowered his arms. *Seven times seven is forty-nine. Seven times eight is—*

'Nearly done…'

He closed his eyes and told himself to keep breathing when she slipped the tape measure around his waist. Her fingers brushed the top of his belt buckle and his eyes flew open…to stare into eyes so blue they transported him to Lake Geneva on a crystal summer's day. A pulse thundered in her throat and her lips parted as if to drag air into lungs that didn't want to work.

Ella might be a professional, but she clearly wasn't as immune as he'd thought. The realisation made him want to swear. The only thing standing between him sweeping her off her feet and into bed was Ella's resolution! If she caved…

No. Operation New Leaf. He *could* resist temptation. He clenched his hands to fists. He *would* resist temptation.

It didn't stop him from wanting to cup her face and exploring that sweet rosebud of a mouth with a slow thoroughness until he'd memorised every millimetre of its enticing lushness.

As if she could read the intent on his face, she swayed towards him. They hovered between breaths, eyes locked…

Then she blinked.

And snapped away.

And the tension holding him tight slackened, and he sagged.

She slipped the tape measure around his hips and he immediately straightened again. 'Fifty-six!' He practically shouted it out.

But she'd already moved away before his groin could thoroughly disgrace him and embarrass them both.

'Fifty-six?' she said, her back to him as she jotted the measurement down.

He rolled his shoulders, stretched his neck to the left and then the right. 'Just a sum I was doing. I was, uh…cooking the books this morning and left a few loose ends.'

'Want me to write it down for you so you don't forget?'

He couldn't look at her. He pulled his phone out with a shake of his head. 'I'll make a note and email it to myself.'

He did too.

The email read: Get a grip!!!

'I thought it might be a forty-two thing.' She turned with a smile that didn't reach her eyes. 'You know—the answer to the ultimate question of life, the universe and everything? From *The Hitchhiker's Guide to the Galaxy*? Douglas Adams?'

He gaped at her.

She stowed the jotted-down measurements in a drawer.

He picked up his jaw. '*The Hitchhiker's Guide to the Galaxy* is my favourite book.'

She swung back. 'Mine too.'

What were the odds? 'Right. First item on the "lunchtime topics of conversation" agenda is favourite sci-fi and fantasy books.'

And just like that she laughed and everything was fine again. 'Let's eat.'

He followed her to the table she'd laid with the prettiest linen cloth embroidered with purple flowers. 'You made this?'

'Repurposed. I found it in a thrift store. The original piece was four times as big as this, and pocked with various holes and stains. I salvaged this piece to make a small tablecloth.'

'Clever.'

She traced one of the purple flowers. She had small hands, but he knew from the equipment she'd just shown him how capable those hands must be. He could imagine...

No, he couldn't. He couldn't imagine anything.

'The embroidery is beautiful. It deserved a second life. Just because something is old and out of fashion or imperfect doesn't mean it should be thrown away.'

He had a feeling that could be a metaphor for life.

'Wine or beer?' she asked him.

'Wine.'

She handed him the bottle to open while she served up a winter vegetable and chorizo frittata that smelled heavenly, along with a green salad and crusty bread. His mouth watered as he gazed at it all.

They ate.

'Dear God, that was good,' he said half an hour later, pushing his plate away after polishing off a second slice of the frittata. 'You're a woman of many talents—a seamstress extraordinaire, a business guru *and* an excellent cook.'

She laughed, and he wanted to make her do it again. It seemed to lift some weight inside her. She'd had so much grief and sadness to deal with in the last year and a half. To now have to battle her family's disapproval of the direction in which she wanted to take her life... His chest clenched. It was too much.

'I'm a lazy cook,' she corrected. 'My MO is to make up a big batch of something and then freeze the leftovers to have for dinner for the rest of the week.'

He stiffened. He shouldn't have had that second slice of frittata. He should've filled up on bread and salad because they wouldn't keep whereas she could've eaten the frittata for—

Her laugh snapped him back. Laughter turned those blue eyes even brighter. 'You need to school your face a little better, Harry. You're too transparent.'

Nobody had accused him of that before.

'Don't feel guilty because you had two slices of the frittata.'

But it could've been another whole night's dinner for her.

'I'm glad you enjoyed it. And notice I said I was lazy, not that I'm penny pinching. It was nice to—'

She broke off with a frown. He stared at that frown and his gut clenched. Nice to *what*?

The furrow in her brow deepened and she shook her head. 'I just hadn't realised—'

She spoke as if to herself and her murmur raised all the fine hairs on his arms. 'Hadn't realised what?'

She started. 'Oh, nothing.'

He raised an eyebrow.

She grimaced. 'Fine! I hadn't realised how circumscribed my life had become.'

'What do you mean?' he said carefully, neutrally. 'Do you mean you've been too focussed on your work?' Or was she talking about the lack of romance in her life?

'I was talking about my social circle.'

The defences he'd started to stake into place wavered.

'The Hawthornes and the Mayberrys—my family and Susie's...'

He noted she said Susie's family, not James's.

'Well, we live in each other's pockets; we're each other's social circle. My mother and Susie's mum have been besties since kindergarten. A tradition James and I continued when we became besties from the cradle.'

Best friends who'd become lovers. He and Ella might share a similar sense of humour, love the same books, and have the same drive and ambition to reach their goals, but it was clear they had wildly different expectations where love was concerned.

'Our parents went into business together before we were born and...' she shrugged '...we consider each other's aunts, uncles, cousins and extended families our own.'

'I guess it's nice,' he offered. 'But I guess it means everyone is in each other's business too.'

One slim shoulder lifted. 'And it's not entirely true that I hadn't realised how limited my social circle had become. I just hadn't realised until today the kind of impact it's had on me. I mean, obviously I have friends outside the family, but most of them have moved away in recent years for work, so it's a weekend trip to visit them. At the moment, The Family—' she said it as if it were capitalised '—almost exclusively makes up my social circle.'

No wonder she felt so suffocated. No wonder she feared she was going to explode. Her life wasn't just circumscribed. It had become too *small*.

She glanced up and forced a smile to her lips. Though he didn't know how he could tell it was forced.

'So today has been a rare treat. To enjoy a meal with someone who's not tied up in knots of grief, or treading far too carefully around me because I've lost my fiancé and they're worried they'll say the wrong thing. It's really nice to be around someone who didn't know James. I'm sorry if that makes me sound hard-hearted, but—'

'You don't sound hard-hearted.' His chest tightened. 'You've every right to enjoy a simple meal with a friend. And every right to enjoy setting up your own business. You shouldn't feel guilty for moving on.'

She glanced down at her hands. 'I know. It's what I tell myself in my more sensible moments.'

It had to be hard, though, when she was surrounded by a family of mourners who couldn't imagine a life for her that didn't involve James.

'It doesn't mean you loved James any less or

miss him any less. But sacrificing your life and happiness to grief would be a sad homage to pay to a man who sounds like a pretty special kind of guy.'

She nodded. 'The funny thing is—'

The twist of lips told him it wasn't funny at all.

'The thing I most miss about James is our friendship. He really was my best friend.'

Most women would have a best friend to help them through the loss of a partner. She'd lost partner and best friend in one fell swoop.

'I need to start making some new friends. I've been so focussed on getting Sew Sensational off the ground that I keep putting off overtures of friendship from people in the sewing community—other teachers at the community college, stallholders at the markets, other vloggers. I've been telling myself I don't have time, but this—' she gestured at what was left of their lunch '—has made me think I need to make the time.'

In that moment he wanted to be her friend more than he could remember wanting anything. He wanted to be her new *best* friend. He opened his mouth—

Don't.

He snapped it shut again. He had to stop being impulsive. He had to tread carefully. He couldn't do anything that would ruin this wedding. He couldn't do anything that might hurt this woman.

He couldn't give the press anything more to talk about.

So he made himself straighten and be sensible. 'I think that's wise. On a lot of levels.'

'Oh?'

God, that eyebrow could slay a man! 'We all need work colleagues. They're the people we bounce ideas off, who help us feel part of a community, whose feedback lets us know if we're on the right track.'

'When we have a wobbly day,' she said slowly, 'they're the ones who remind us of all the reasons we love what we love.'

She'd had no one to help her through the wobbly days. He couldn't even... 'I'd never have won a world championship without the support of my team—people who believed in me.' Some days he'd kept going simply for them. They'd all worked as hard as he had.

She stared as if his words were gold. He ordered himself not to let it go to his head. 'Also, if the family sees you making new friends, it'll show them you're moving on in positive ways.'

Behind the blue of her eyes her mind raced. 'And then they'll worry about me less...might focus more on Susie and the wedding. And maybe...'

'And maybe it will help them move on too,' he finished for her.

He could tell from the expression in her eyes

how much she wanted that for them, wanted to see them happy again.

'We don't do this haphazardly, Ella. We create an agenda.' She needed to broaden her world.

Two beats passed, before she gave a wary nod. 'Okay.'

'How's this for a start? Some time during this coming week drop into conversation with your mother that you had lunch or something with one of your fellow sewing teachers—and make sure you have that lunch. Maybe you can tell Susie you attended a gathering of fellow vloggers or...'

'A sew-along held by the local sewing guild,' she said, taking up where he left off. 'I've been a member forever, but I haven't attended an event in...' She trailed off. 'I should be making connections with anyone who might be interested in my sewing school.'

She sent him the smallest of smiles, but it shattered every single barricade he'd tried to put in place.

'Plus it'd be fun.'

And it was clear she'd not had enough of that in her life in recent times. When it came to fun, he was the master. He sent her a grin that made her blink. 'Speaking of fun... Can we go pull those sewing machines apart yet?'

CHAPTER FOUR

ELLA WALKED HARRY through the servicing of the sewing machines, and his genuine enjoyment further lightened the weight that had been pressing on her heart for eighteen long months.

She was beginning see the missteps she'd made. For a start, she shouldn't have given those twelve months after James's death to the family business. She should've confided her plans to the family *much* sooner. Maybe then they wouldn't have misinterpreted her growing restlessness as a sign of grief.

She'd then spent too much of her leisure time with them in an attempt to reassure them they weren't losing her. Harry was right. They needed to see her moving on and being happy rather than stressed and resentful. They needed to see her making friends and laughing more, settling into her new world. Once they could see her doing that, maybe they'd start to trust her.

'You know, it's not just me—'

She started at the same time as he said, 'You know what else I think you should do?'

They broke off at the same time. 'You first,' she said. Everything he'd suggested so far had been solid gold and she was curious to hear his next suggestion.

'I think you ought to start dating again.'

His words shocked her so much she leapt out of her chair and strode around the drafting table. 'No way.'

He folded his arms. 'Why not?'

'So many reasons.' She strode back and took her seat again, because pacing seemed like an overreaction. 'So *so* many reasons.'

'Give me one.'

'I'll give you three.'

He leaned back and folded his arms as if he had all the time in the world. 'Hit me with the first one.'

She fought an entirely alien urge to thump him. 'I'm not ready.' How was that for starters? She and James might not have been seeing eye to eye in those last few weeks, but it didn't mean she wanted to start seeing someone else.

His face gentled. 'Ella, it's been eighteen months.'

'I know how long it's been, but it doesn't change the fact that I'm not ready to fall in love again.' There had been days when she'd missed James so much she'd thought the ache would kill her. She didn't want to think about men, she didn't want to think about relationships. She didn't want to think about any of it.

'Who said anything about falling in love?'

The pulse in her throat missed a beat.

'Dating doesn't have to be about falling in love. It can just be about having fun. I'm living proof of that, aren't I?'

If it was so much fun, why didn't he look happier about it?

'Dating can be a casual thing, a social outlet.'

She pursed her lips. 'Casual?'

He nodded, though she suspected he was trying not to laugh at her consternation.

She glanced away, wrinkling her nose. 'The thing is, Harry, I haven't dated casually in my life. I don't even know how that works.'

He stared at her before pursing his own lips. 'That's right, childhood sweethearts.'

Bingo.

'It's easy.'

Sounded damn terrifying to her.

'You bump into someone—maybe at the markets—it might even be someone you sort of know or have seen around. Anyway, you share a joke or a stray comment about the goods for sale, and he—or she—asks if you'd like to go for a cup of coffee some time. You say *That'd be lovely*, and you exchange phone numbers. You set a time, meet for coffee and have a nice time.'

He made it sound easy.

'What if that person wants more? What if they're looking for a serious relationship?'

'During that first coffee date, you make it clear what you're looking for and where you stand.'

She mulled that over. 'So if he's looking for serious he doesn't ring me again. And if he isn't...' She frowned harder. 'We what? Become friends?'

A low laugh shook through him. 'You really are new at this, aren't you? If you enjoy each other's company and like the look of each other...'

He stared at her expectantly...spread his hands. She shot back out of her chair. 'Oh, God, you're talking about sex.' She stalked around her drafting table, twice.

'Is it really so shocking?'

'Yes.' She glared. Though it wasn't. Not really. She'd been thinking about sex a lot. Even though she'd been doing her best to ignore it.

He studied her, lips pursed. She felt like a butterfly on the end of a pin. 'Do you find sex without commitment morally reprehensible?'

'No.' She sighed and took her seat again. 'Casual sex sounds great in theory.' She nibbled the inside of her cheek. 'Really great,' she murmured. And then shook herself, straightened, ordered her cheeks to stop burning. 'It makes me feel guilty though, because...' She trailed off with a grimace.

He nodded to let her know he understood.

She forced herself to take a slow deep breath, in

a measured *adult* way. 'But I'm young and healthy and in my sexual prime. It's normal for someone my age to miss sex and want—'

Too much information! Harry was no longer looking at her. He didn't need, or want, to hear this.

She folded her arms. 'Okay, you've made your point.' Time to move on. 'Reason number two.'

He motioned with his hands. 'Hit me with it.'

'Me dating would send the family into a spin. They'd find it confronting.'

His eyes narrowed. 'The family doesn't get to decide when you're ready to start dating again. That's your decision.'

'And yours apparently.' She rolled her eyes. 'It's clearly what you're pushing me towards.'

'Not pushing, just reminding you of the benefits.'

Sex.

She stared at him and then reefed her gaze away. Played with a spare bobbin she hadn't packed away yet. She definitely shouldn't think about sex and Harry in the same sentence.

'The thing is, Ella, they *don't* get a say in it. The other thing is...'

She glanced up.

'One day you will meet a guy who makes your heart beat faster, who you can imagine settling down with and—'

'*Not* going to happen!' The words emerged

more violently than she meant them to, and his eyebrows shot up. Her shoulders ached and her temples throbbed. Maybe the family were right and she ought to mourn James forever. Maybe that was the right thing to do.

He studied her for several long moments. 'You might not be able to imagine it at the moment, but… What about kids? Don't you want those? I mean, I know you don't have to be in a committed relationship to have them, but the single-parent route is tough.'

She'd be lying if she said she didn't want children.

'I think, at some point in the future, white picket fences will feature on your horizon once again. The family might find that difficult to accept at first, but you'll be making this hypothetical guy's life a whole lot easier if you date a few transitional guys first.'

'Bring home a few frogs for them to scare off first?' The thought made her smile. She wasn't in the market for love right now, and maybe she never would be. Yet Harry's strategy was still a sound one.

'What's reason number three?'

She gestured at her workshop. 'My main focus is getting Sew Sensational established.'

He folded his arms. 'You can still find the time to date.'

'I could find the time if I *wanted* to date, but I

don't. This is going to sound selfish, but I don't want to pander to any guy's ego at the moment. I only want to focus on what's important to me.'

'And that's building Sew Sensational?'

She hesitated. 'I've had first-hand experience at the kind of curveball life can throw at you, Harry.'

He lifted a hand as if to reach across and squeeze hers. Instead, he picked up a nearby spool of thread and turned it over and over in his fingers.

She forced her mind from his fingers and back to the conversation. 'If I can make a success of Sew Sensational, that means I'll always have something in my life that's mine, that can't be taken away from me.'

'Something you can fall back on if life goes pear-shaped again.'

She nodded. He did understand. 'Sew Sensational, Susie's wedding, the family…' she chewed the inside of her cheek '…and making a few new friends are all I have time for at the moment.'

Those fingers tapped against the spool of thread. 'Guys can be friends too.'

He almost sounded as if he were putting himself forward for the job. She folded her arms, but she didn't know if it was to protect herself from that thought or to temper the pounding of her heart. 'We've talked an awful lot about me, Harry. Can we talk about you for a moment?'

He rolled his shoulders, shifted on his seat. 'What do you want to know?'

'You said you're currently giving dating and romance a wide berth.'

'That's right.'

His eyes narrowed and he said the words carefully…and clearly. Was he worried she might challenge him, try and change his mind? He shouldn't. She'd meant it when she said she didn't have room in her life for any guy at the moment.

'I've shared why romance won't be featuring on my horizon any time in the near future, but what's your reason?'

He continued to stare at her with narrowed eyes and she suddenly realised why. She sat back. 'You don't trust me.' The realisation stung.

'It's not personal.'

Seriously? How else was she supposed to take it? She kept her chin high. 'I suppose you've had more than one woman sell a tell-all exposé to the tabloids. I guess you've learned to be cautious.'

Which was sad and awful.

'My gut tells me I can trust you.'

But it was clear his gut had led him astray in the past.

He swore softly. 'It feels mean-spirited to not answer your question when you've been so open with me.'

She waved that away. 'Don't worry about it.'

'No. I *am* going to trust you. I'm not an idiot. I can tell when a person is genuine or not.'

Her gaze speared back to his.

His eyes flashed. 'I'm not going to let them take that away from me. Sometimes it's worth the risk—even if you do find yourself mistaken and disappointed. I refuse to turn into some sad and lonely cynic.'

'That would be a tragedy,' she agreed, a smile lifting through her. 'I won't tell the world your secrets, Harry. They're safe with me.'

His gaze didn't waver from hers. 'I believe you.'

Something in her chest hitched. What was it about this man that made her feel so empowered?

'I'm wanting to partner with a charity called Bright Directions. It helps teenagers struggling with depression. My plan is to set up ski clinics to give these kids a chance to experience a week on the slopes, and an opportunity to build new skills that will boost their self-esteem.'

She stared at him, momentarily lost for words. 'That's...it's a gorgeous idea.'

He gave a half-grin—a little abashed and a lot self-conscious—and she had to fight an impulse to hug him. 'Lily's going to head the programme up for me, and she's really excited about it.'

'Of course she is.' Who wouldn't be?

'But the charity is pretty conservative, and the trustees are wary about partnering with someone who has developed a reputation as a playboy. They want their name to be synonymous with respect-ability, and anyone they partner with needs to be role-model material.'

Ah.

'I mean, I have the connections in the skiing world, and I have the money…'

'But I'm guessing pictures of you with what seems like a different girl on your arm every week, looking as if your entire life is a party, isn't exactly convincing them that you're serious.'

'No.'

'But if those pictures were to stop…you might be able to convince them that you've turned over a new leaf?'

'It's the plan.' And then he shook his head. 'It's my own fault. I've played up my reputation to the tabloids because I've found it amusing.' He leaned back, expelled a breath. 'The thing is, I've never been interested in having a serious relationship. I love playing the field and can't imagine settling down with one woman.'

He actually shuddered. Clearly white picket fences were the stuff of nightmares for him.

'So I've exaggerated certain aspects of my be-haviour to send that message loud and clear.' He was silent for a moment. 'I'm not built for the long haul. Some people aren't, you know? I think it's best to be honest about these things.'

'Absolutely,' she agreed. 'But now all of that ex-aggeration has come back to bite you on the nose.'

'So it would seem.'

'And that was your reason for avoiding the scary ladies' table on Friday night.'

'That's exactly the kind of table I need to avoid if I'm to rehabilitate my image.'

'Are you finding it hard?'

'Not in the way you think. I don't crave a new woman on my arm every week, and I don't need a calendar full of parties. People seem to forget that I run a successful business, that I work hard. Most of the events I attend these days are for business purposes.'

That made sense. 'So what *do* you find hard about it?'

'Staying on my guard. No longer teasing the media—that's hard to resist. It had become a bit of a game, a bit of fun.'

Because at heart he was a fun-loving guy who didn't feel the need to explain himself to anyone.

'Martin's wedding is a godsend. It's pulled me out of the limelight and is giving me the chance to prove myself.'

She tapped a finger against her lips. 'And if we're to drag this wedding out of the doldrums, you're going to be too busy to be snapped doing much else.' She straightened. Tit for tat. 'Well, Harry, if there's anything I can do to help, let me know.'

He blinked. 'That's nice of you.'

Guys can be friends too.

She moistened her lips. 'Well, as I said… I need a few new friends.'

His eyes throbbed. 'If you believe what the papers say, I can't just be friends with a woman.'

'I don't care what the papers say. I care what you say. Can you just be friends with a woman?'

He leaned in close and she saw he had lighter flecks in his irises, the colour of gold. 'Yes.'

'Then maybe we can be friends.' In the short term. It wouldn't last. She wouldn't see him once the wedding was over, but he could be…a transitional friend maybe.

One side of his mouth hooked up. 'I'd like that, Ella, but I'm not going to be your new BFF. You have priors for falling in love with those.'

Her jaw dropped. And then she choked back a splutter of laughter. *'Once!'* She held up a single finger. 'Once does not make me a serial faller-in-love with my BFFs. It's not a pattern.'

He grinned and held out his hand.

She grinned back and shook it.

CHAPTER FIVE

'OKAY, SO TELL me how it went.'

It was Friday night, and Ella watched Harry as he unpacked a Chinese takeaway—honey prawns, Mongolian lamb, fried rice and stir-fry vegetables all appeared on the table before her.

'Which part?' And then she gestured at the food. 'How many people were you planning to feed?'

'I couldn't decide what I wanted. And I figured you'd find a use for any leftovers.'

She grabbed plates and cutlery and tried to not dwell on the fact that it was sort of sweet of him to make sure she had leftovers.

There was nothing *sort of* about it. Harry *was* a sweet guy, period.

'As I told you on Wednesday night—' when they'd chatted on the phone '—it was lovely.'

After teaching her class on Tuesday night, she'd gone for coffee and dessert with two of her fellow teachers at the community college. 'We talked shop, and our bigger creative goals, and it was...'

'Yes?' he prompted, a spring roll halfway to his mouth.

Spring rolls? Where were they? Spotting them, she reached for one and bit into it, trying to find the right words. 'Invigorating. Freeing. Guilt-free. Well, not if you count the chocolate lava cake I had.'

He huffed out a laugh that warmed her to her toes. 'You don't need to worry about your weight, Ella. You look great.'

For a fraction of a moment their gazes caught and clung. They both looked away at the same time. She rattled back into speech. 'I told them about my Sew Sensational plans and they asked intelligent questions, challenged me on a few points.'

He set his spring roll down, his brow pleating. 'Challenged?'

She pointed at his plate. 'You want to eat that while it's warm. They're really good. And, yeah, challenged. Joy teaches advertising and thinks I need a more distinctive logo. Aleeta is an artist who immediately started doodling potential logos…and said she could create a banner for my website and YouTube channel too. Neither of them liked my current one.'

He thrust out his jaw. 'What's wrong with it?'

'No, they're right. It's an amateur job—just something I whipped up as a placeholder that I've never got around to updating.' She helped herself to the honey prawns. 'We're going to work out a quid pro quo arrangement where we can help each other out without cash actually changing hands.'

'Sounds great.'

'We're making Tuesday dessert night a regular thing.' She handed him the prawns. 'I'm really looking forward to next week. I enjoyed it more than I have any outing in a long time.'

If it hadn't been for his prodding, she'd have missed out on it. Catching her eye, he sent her a grin—one that made the right side of his mouth hook up in a devil-may-care kind of way, and her pulse did a little jig.

Be sensible. Harry. Friend. That's all.

'And yesterday I popped into one of my favourite fabric warehouses and bumped into one of the stallholders from the markets. We started chatting and ended up hunkering down in the pattern section for an hour.'

He ladled food to his plate. 'That's not something you'd normally do?'

'No.' She frowned. 'And now I'm wondering why not. I can't remember why it always seemed so important to get back to the workshop asap. It was nice to connect creatively with someone on a work level.' It had reinforced her love for what she was doing. It had helped to strengthen her belief in herself, confidence that her family's scepticism had battered. 'Not only was it fun, but creatively instructive.'

'Sounds brilliant *and* productive.'

It had been.

His gaze raked her face and he gave a nod. 'You look better. More relaxed.'

She refused to read anything into the warmth of his eyes. Harry had made it very clear he wasn't interested in her in that way. And she wasn't interested in him either.

'I feel better,' she admitted. 'Not so tightly wound…like I might explode at a moment's notice.' Which was a relief. 'I hadn't realised I'd fallen into such a negative holding pattern. No wonder the family have been so concerned about me…and sceptical about what I'm trying to do here.' Her frown deepened. 'You've been a god-send, Harry.'

He stared and then laughed. 'You could try and look a bit happier about that.'

'Oh, I didn't mean—'

'I know what you meant.'

He grinned and she couldn't help grinning back.

'Did you manage to slip the dessert date into conversation with your mother.'

'And Susie too.'

'Way to go, Ella.'

They high-fived. Both her mother and Susie had been surprised, but they'd made all the right noises. There'd been consternation threaded beneath the encouragement too, though. She reminded herself this was a process—change didn't happen overnight.

They ate in silence for a while. Eventually she pushed her plate away and patted her stomach. She'd eaten far more than she should have. 'So I've had a bit of inspiration on the cheering-them-up front.'

He pushed his plate away too. 'I'm all ears.'

'Beer?'

'Love one,' he said, rising to help her clear away.

She grabbed a beer for him and a soda for herself. 'It occurred to me that if I hadn't realised the negative patterns I'd fallen into, maybe they don't realise their own. I know them seeing me being more cheerful and relaxed and enthusiastic is going to help ease their worry—' she crossed her fingers '—but we need to shake them out of their negative ways too.'

'You have some thoughts on how we can do that?'

'What if we get them doing the things they used to love doing? Things they've stopped doing since James died.'

He straightened. 'I like it. What kind of things are we talking here?'

'Karaoke.'

His eyes lit up. 'No way.'

'Yes way. The whole family is crazy about karaoke.'

'You can sing?'

That made her laugh. 'I didn't say that.'

'What else?'

'The dads used to love going to the baseball.'

'Right.' He clapped his hands. 'I know Martin and Susie said they didn't want hen and stag parties, that the week in Malaysia is going to be one big party and more than enough.'

Ella rolled her eyes. 'Yeah, and like a whole week of partying doesn't put the pressure on us or anything.'

He grinned at that. 'We're up for the challenge, Ella.'

He made her believe they were—that *she* was.

'But now I'm going to organise a boys' day to the baseball prior to flying out and I think you should host a girls' day. What do Susie and the mums love?'

'Susie is mad about musicals.'

He tapped idle fingers against his glass. 'Don't you have dress fittings for Susie and the mums soon?'

'Not until the weekend before we fly out.' Which was only three weeks away.

'You could do the fittings and then have a party afterwards, play soundtracks from musicals during the afternoon, host a musical-related trivia game. You want to play songs from the upbeat musicals, though, not the mournful ones.'

Susie would love it. And it could be fun. '*Grease* and *The Sound of Music*,' she murmured.

'*Hairspray* and *Mamma Mia*.'

That made her grin. 'I love a man who knows his musicals.' Dear God, why did she have to go and use the L word? She rushed on, hoping he hadn't noticed. 'We'll have champagne and nibbles…and I'll organise something fun.' She'd have to put her thinking cap on, because she didn't want it to be anything that reminded anyone of James.

She twisted her hands together. 'I want to ask you something. And I need you to tell me the truth.'

He crossed his heart, instantly alert.

They'd known one another for such a short time, but she trusted him. It made her frown. *Be careful, Ella.* She couldn't come to rely too much on Harry. She couldn't replace one set of negative behaviours with another.

She pressed her hands together. 'I've long suspected that, before any group event, certain family members put their heads together and come up with a plan for how to manage me.'

He'd had his right ankle resting at his left knee, but his foot slammed to the floor now. He stared at her.

'Do you think I'm wrong?' She wanted to be wrong.

He mulled her words over. 'The widows' table...it was planned?'

'I think so.'

He set his beer to the table. 'It's worse than I thought.'

'I'm thinking of turning the tables on them. I'm thinking of ringing Mum and Auntie Rachel the day before the dress fittings to tell them we need to make sure it's a fun day for Susie.' She chewed her lip. 'But...is that mean-spirited?'

His brow pleated. 'You want Susie to have a fun day, don't you?'

'Of course!'

'And you want the mums to help you achieve that.' He shook his head. 'That's just you stating the outcome you want. And it sends them a subtle message that they no longer need to *manage* you. It's neither mean-spirited nor unkind.'

His words gave her heart.

'The thing is, Ella, while they're focussing on you, they don't have to address their own sense of loss.'

Her eyes started to burn. She knew how much they were hurting. She wished she could wipe all of their pain away. 'I just want to see them happy again.'

He reached across and gripped her hand. 'You will.'

She clung tight to that promise.

He abruptly released her and she had an awful

feeling she'd been gazing at him in adoration. She swallowed. If she had been, it had only been on account of her family, *not* for any other reason.

'Ready to try your waistcoat *toile* on?' She was looking forward to seeing the look on his face when he saw it.

'Lead the way.'

She took him across to the cutting table and whisked off the cover on her dressmaking model.

His jaw dropped. And then a grin threatened to split his face in two. 'Where did you get this?'

He reached out to touch the fabric—cartoon skiers made their way down snowy slopes on a light blue background. The fabric was fun, light-hearted and she'd thought of him the moment she'd seen it. She hadn't been able to resist.

'This isn't a mock-up. It's brilliant!'

'There's nothing fancy about it,' she warned. 'The fabric is an inexpensive cotton. It's what we call a wearable *toile*. The wedding waistcoats will be in fine wool and patterned silk—the sort of fabrics I'd prefer to not handle too much, which is why I want to get the fit right on these first. Now let's see if it fits.'

He'd worn a white button-down business shirt as she'd ordered, and he shrugged off his jacket—black leather, of course—to don the waistcoat. She couldn't help but laugh when he turned. 'It suits you. Now let's check the fit.'

She walked around him, smoothing the fabric

across his back. 'I thought I might've made it a little big across here.' She tried to ignore the heat scorching her fingertips, but it was impossible. Harry's heat was a living, breathing thing that took on a life of its own. She swallowed. 'But the fit looks good.'

She walked around him again, ordered her gaze to not linger on taut buttocks in form-fitting jeans. She risked smoothing a hand across his shoulders again. The man felt like heaven.

She curled her fingers into her palms. *Stop it.* The guy was off limits. *She* was off limits.

She told herself to look away, but her eyes refused to obey. His chest looked so very broad and muscled—the most inviting thing she'd seen in a *very* long time. She could imagine being plastered against it and—

She took a hasty step back, hands on hips—her fingers digging into the fleshy area just below her waistline with a death grip that would probably leave bruises. *Be professional.* 'How does it feel? Any spots where it feels too snug or a bit loose?'

He shook his head. 'It's perfect.'

He didn't look at her, stared instead at the fabric, and she dragged in a breath. While she might be in danger of getting all het up, he was completely oblivious. Which was just as well.

A bad taste coated her tongue all the same. The simple truth was she wasn't the kind of woman to tempt a man like Harry.

Also—*hello*—he had a noble goal. She couldn't do anything that would mess that up for him.

And she couldn't afford any more slip-ups that would give her family further reason to think her incapable of making a sensible decision. She gestured. 'There's a full-length mirror in the corner.'

He marched across and stared at her handiwork, moving this way and that before meeting her gaze. 'You're a magician.'

That made her laugh.

He froze, and then he swung around, his entire face coming alive. 'Can you make me more of these? Ski themed, but suitable to wear with business suits? And maybe an even fancier one for evening wear?'

She shrugged. 'Sure.'

He turned back to the mirror, tugged gently on the hem of the waistcoat. 'Because these will attract attention.'

Attention?

He raised an eyebrow. 'I'm not normally one to toot my own horn, but I am an A-lister…'

She suddenly realised what he was talking about. Her heart thudded so hard she could barely speak. 'You'd…? No way!' He'd endorse her brand?

'You might not get your fashion expo, but there are other ways to get your name out there.'

Her mind raced. This was ten times better than the expo! Once the press took photos of Harry in those waistcoats she'd be flooded with orders, and the Sew Sensational brand would be established.

If her family could see Sew Sensational making a splash, could finally see its potential, that would help alleviate their anxiety levels where she was concerned, surely? And free them up to focus on happier things like Susie's wedding.

'I watched some of your YouTube videos through the week.'

She bumped back to earth, wiped suddenly damp palms down her jeans. 'And?'

'You're a natural on camera—personable, enthusiastic, super encouraging...' His eyes darkened. 'And a little bit flirty.'

Her mouth dried. 'Flirty?'

'You're like the Nigella Lawson of the sewing world. Your passion for your subject shines through.'

Flirty? Did that mean he thought her just the tiniest bit sexy?

'You're a born teacher.'

A lump lodged in her throat. He really thought so?

'For God's sake, you made me want to learn how to sew!'

That made her laugh.

He shifted his weight from one foot to the other. 'You sometimes have guests on your channel.'

He raised an eyebrow and spread his hands. Her pulse went haywire. 'No way,' she breathed.

'Yes, way.'

If she had him on as a guest, her ratings would skyrocket.

'You could do a segment on waistcoats featuring me—we could talk about how the idea for them came about. And I'd be your model.'

Her mind raced as ideas dive-bombed her. 'Oh!' She glanced at him. 'Wouldn't it interfere with your image makeover?' Because no matter how good this would be for Sew Sensational, she wasn't doing anything that would hurt his charity efforts.

'I can't see how. It'd probably help. I—' He broke off and eyed her warily. 'I mean, as long as I keep my shirt on. I…'

'I'm not going to ask you to go shirtless, Harry.' No matter how much she might want to. 'It's not that kind of channel.'

'You interested, then? Do you think it'd help?'

'I think it's inspired, and it's a sure-fire way of getting my name out there.' It was a lot to ask, though. 'As long as you don't mind?'

'Are you kidding? I mean, I get free bespoke waistcoats, right?'

She found herself grinning. 'You absolutely do.'

He grinned down at her. 'I'm on a roll; here's another great idea. I'm attending a swish do in a couple of weeks' time where I'll be schmoozing with the trustees of Bright Directions, and doing my best to prove I'm someone they want to be associated with. That's where I want to wear one of the waistcoats.'

He leaned down towards her and she could smell leather and amber and every good thing.

'Ella, if you went as my date, you'd be able to talk about your work to the kind of people who set, not just fashion trends, but all kinds of trends.'

Her heart hammered into her throat and she couldn't utter a word.

'Interested?'

'Very.' She couldn't get her hopes up though, because... 'Again, what about your no-dating policy? Won't the media and the trustees get the wrong idea if you turn up with a woman on your arm?'

'That depends on the woman, and I suspect dating a woman like you will only help my image, not harm it.' He gave a single hard nod. 'Right, that's a date, then.' And then he waggled his eyebrows. 'But not a *date* date.'

Absolutely not a *date* date.

'Can I ask another favour?'

She started to laugh then. This man was helping put her brand on the map. 'You really truly can.'

'Will you teach me to sew?'

She had a feeling her grin was in danger of splitting her face in two. She gestured across the room. 'Choose your machine, my friend.'

Friend. She repeated the word over and over in her mind.

CHAPTER SIX

'THIS IS WHERE you live?'

Harry bit back a grin at Ella's astonishment. Holborn House was pretty impressive. 'It belongs to my mother—it's where she stays when she's in Sydney.' He punched in the security code for the double wrought-iron gates. 'I have my own place in Woolloomooloo.' But Holborn House was where Lily currently lived.

'It's been in the family for three generations.' A drive lined with date palms led to an enormous Victorian mansion with expansive views of the harbour. 'This is what a mining empire buys you.'

He'd meant to say the words with wry mockery, but an edge of bitterness tinged them too and he could've kicked himself when the weight of Ella's gaze settled on him. She didn't ask a single question, though, didn't probe or pry. He rolled his shoulders. 'My mother works too hard to enjoy the spoils of the family's wealth.'

He parked the car. In the sudden silence the engine clicked and ticked as it started to cool. 'This was where I grew up before my parents divorced. Afterwards, my mother threw herself into running the family's holdings.' And had become a virtual stranger.

'And your father?'

'Couldn't be seen for the dust he left in his wake.' It had been demoralising how hard and fast his father had run. 'Lily and I were shunted off to boarding school.'

It had felt as if he and Lily had lost both parents in one fell swoop. His hands gripped the steering wheel so hard his fingers started to ache. Lily had lost not one, but two families. It had sent her into a spiral that had almost resulted in her death. That was what this house represented to him now. He forced a smile to frozen lips, rolled his eyes. 'They were the very best schools, though, of course.'

One soft hand curled over his on the steering wheel, and he found himself turning, found himself in danger of falling into clear blue eyes. 'All the wealth in the world is no comfort when your world comes tumbling down, Harry. You lost your whole way of life through no fault of your own. It must've been the most awful time.' She stared at the house. 'My family is driving me batty at the moment, but I'm incredibly lucky to have them.'

He squeezed her hand before leaping out of the car and racing around to open her door. 'Come and see the view,' he said, changing the subject. 'It's glorious.'

Lily met them on the terrace. Taking Ella's hand, she tugged her inside. 'There's something I'm dying to show you.'

He trailed behind. And then pulled up short at the sight that greeted them. Spread across one of the large sofas in the formal living room was *a wedding dress*!

What the hell...? His hands clenched and un-clenched. He'd sensed Viggo was trouble from the first moment he'd met him, but Lily couldn't be hoping to marry the guy. And even if Viggo were serious, surely Lily wouldn't contemplate...

'It's my mother's wedding dress.'

Her mother's? He sagged.

'Aunt Claudia sent on some of my parents' things from the Brisbane house last week, this among them. The moment I saw it...'

She trailed off with a shrug and he wrapped an arm around her shoulders. 'That's a hell of a find. It must be nice to have it.'

'It is.'

She leaned into him and some of his anxiety eased.

'But there are a few marks and tears, and I don't know what I ought to do about it. I was hoping Ella could point me in the right direction.'

Ella inspected the dress. 'It's exquisite,' she said eventually, reverence in her voice. 'The damage is only minor. This could easily be restored to its former glory.' She swung to them with a smile that made his heart beat hard, her curls dancing all around her face. 'It's pure nineteen-eighties over-the-top fabulousness, probably influenced by Princess Di's dress.'

'Would you like to see a picture of my mother in it?'

'Yes, please!'

Harry fixed drinks while Lily raced off to get the photo. 'I'm sorry Lily wants to talk shop. You probably get sick of people asking you about stuff like this.'

'Nonsense! I live for stuff like this.' She gestured towards the gown. 'It's a real privilege to see something like that. The workmanship is out of this world.'

Lily returned with a framed photograph and the two women oohed and ahhed and he couldn't say why, but those two heads bent close together—one dark and one fair—had a strange warmth stretching through his chest.

'Okay, so I want to ask your advice on one point, and then I'll stop pestering you about sewing stuff.'

'I *love* sewing stuff and you're not pestering me.'

She was utterly glorious, he decided in that moment—enthusiastic and warm. And kind.

'Would it be possible, do you think, to rework this dress into…' Lily's hands fluttered. 'Into the dress of my dreams?'

'Why all this sudden interest in weddings?' he barked.

Lily glanced at him and rolled her eyes. 'Maybe because my mother's wedding dress has suddenly turned up and started me thinking about such things.' She peered at him. 'Why, what's wrong?'

Her question made him feel like an idiot. He grimaced. 'In my head you're still fifteen and...'

'Oh, Lord, you're hilarious,' Ella said. 'I bet he was a nightmare when you first started dating, Lily.'

Both women laughed and turned back to the dress, ignoring him. He had a feeling he deserved to be ignored.

'Tell me about your dream dress,' Ella said.

'I do love the old Edwardian style.'

'Ooh, me too.'

They started throwing around ideas, discussing pros and cons. He looked up Edwardian wedding dresses on his phone, because he had no idea what they were talking about. He stared at the pictures and nodded. Nice.

'Now, say if this is too much,' Lily said, 'but Harrison told me about the waistcoats and it's what gave me the idea.'

He immediately transferred his attention back to the women.

'Ella, would you consider helping me to make that dream dress...and in return we could film the process for your channel?'

Ella went ramrod straight. 'Are you serious? Lily, I don't have specific expertise in this area. You could take it to a couture designer and—'

'I don't want some big-name designer. I want you. I want you to teach me how to make that dress myself. It might sound strange, but it'll make me feel closer to my mother. And one day when I do get married, wearing this dress will make me feel like a part of her is with me.' She blinked a few times before rushing back into speech. 'I watch your YouTube channel religiously. I saw the episode where you made that formal gown. I saw the wedding dress in your studio. I love the way you teach and I know with you I'd have the confidence to tackle something like this.'

'That's a lovely thing to say,' Ella whispered.

'Please say you'll do it.' Lily leaned towards her, hands pressed together in an unconscious plea.

Harry held his breath and waited for Ella's answer. *Please say yes.*

'Oh, Lily, I'd be honoured.'

Lily threw her arms around her and Harry couldn't get the grin off his face.

They shared a delicious roast dinner and the conversation didn't have a chance to flag. Ella asked about the plans they were hoping to make with Bright Directions, and Lily described their programme in detail. When she told Ella that she'd had an eating disorder in her teens and that was why working with this particular charity meant

so much to her, he nearly swallowed his tongue.
She so rarely spoke about it.

His hands clenched about his cutlery. He had
to make this partnership with Bright Directions
happen.

'Between the two of you I'm sure you'll win
them over. It's a brilliant initiative.'

Ella's smile made him feel as if he could achieve
anything.

'Now tell me about Malaysia. Harrison tells me
the plans were sprung on you both without notice.'

Ella told her about the upcoming wedding and
the scheduled week in Malaysia. She even told
her that it meant she'd now be missing the fashion expo she had such hopes for.

Waistcoats...? Wedding dresses...? Harry suddenly clapped his hands. 'Could you turn Malaysia to your advantage?'

Both women turned to him.

'Could you do some Sew Sensational filming
on location? A special feature on...' He grappled
for an idea. This world was so new to him. 'Something beach themed?'

'Oh, my God,' Lily squealed. 'Do a couple of
your Fast Fashion sessions on...'

'Three things to make from a sarong,' Ella said,
her whole face coming alive. 'Everyone has a couple of old sarongs in their wardrobe.' But a moment later she sobered. 'There won't be time. Not
with the wedding and—'

'We could stay an extra week.'

Lily bounced. 'Say yes! And let me join you for part of it. I could be your guinea pig learner sewer who shows everyone how easy it can be.'

Ella bit her lip. 'I really shouldn't take so much time off.'

'You won't be taking time off. You'll be working,' he pointed out. 'What will you be missing here?'

She tapped a finger to her lips. 'It'll be mid-semester break at college, which means no classes for a few weeks, and I'd miss one market day.' She paused. 'But for something like this...'

Please say yes.

She glanced up and must've seen that command in his eyes because she grinned, excitement alive in her eyes. 'Let's do it.'

He wanted to punch the air in victory.

'I meant to ask earlier. How did the family barbecue go on Sunday?'

Harry glanced briefly at Ella before turning his eyes back to the road. The evening had been one of the most enjoyable he could remember. She'd assured him she'd be happy to catch the train home, but he'd insisted on driving her. Just as he'd insisted on collecting her earlier in the evening.

'Um...'

He stiffened.

'There were some...*uncomfortable* moments.'

'Okay...' He didn't know whether to press her or not.

'The first was when Dad made a comment about what I was wearing—said something about it being bright and cheerful.'

He'd seen what she'd planned to wear, primarily because she'd been in the process of making the skirt the last time he'd had a sewing lesson—a long velvet number in the most astonishing shade of yellow. She'd planned to team it with an apple-green long-sleeved tee.

'And I made the mistake of saying, "Harry told me all I needed was purple shoes and an orange belt and I'd look like a rainbow vomited over me."'

He barked out a laugh. When Ella decided to do colour, she *really* did colour. He might tease her about it, but those bright colours suited her.

'So then came the third degree—when had I seen you and why? How much time were we spending together?'

'What did you say?'

'Told them the truth—that we were bridesmaid and best man and as such needed to put our heads together about certain things. It sort of eased their minds.'

It'd *sort of* do them good to start thinking about Ella seeing other men, but he didn't say that out loud.

'Sounds like you handled it well.'

'Maybe, maybe not.'

Her sigh speared into his chest. He glanced at her again. 'If that's the worst the afternoon held—'

'I told them James knew about my plans to strike out on my own with Sew Sensational.'

His hands tightened around the steering wheel at the mention of James. 'Wow, okay.'

'I didn't plan to. I just *blurted it out*. I wanted them to know my decision hadn't come out of the blue. So then came another third degree—why hadn't I told them this before? What did James think about it?' From the corner of his eye he saw her fold her arms. 'I told them he was disappointed, that he didn't want me leaving the business.'

He winced.

'And I told them he also knew I had my heart set on it.'

She stared straight out to the front, her lips pressed in a tight line. He wanted to take her hand and offer her comfort. 'What happened then?'

'They all went quiet. So I added that I've never felt more vocationally fulfilled as I have these last six months and I wish they could just be happy for me.' She swung to him suddenly. 'Do you think I've wrecked everything? Do you think I've ruined the wedding and—?'

'Absolutely not!' She might've shaken them up but... 'You're refusing to allow them to keep casting you in the role of tragic victim. Confronting for them, no doubt, but also positive as it removes you as a constant source of concern. You don't need to feel guilty for any of that, Ella.'

She rubbed a hand across her chest. 'I hope you're right.'

He moistened his lips. 'James's accident...what happened? Do you mind me asking? I know he drowned, but...'

She was quiet for a moment. 'He sometimes swam laps in the mornings before work. We lived in a little flat in Cremorne and he'd use the nearby ocean baths.' She paused, her hands gripped tightly in her lap. 'As far as we can make out, he slipped and hit his head on the rocks...knocked himself out before falling into the water.'

His heart burned.

'It was still dark...nobody saw it happen...'

And a life was snuffed out, just like that. He reached across and squeezed her hand. 'I'm sorry.'

'Me too.' She squeezed back and then straightened. 'Now, enough about me. Lily had an eating disorder. That... I can only imagine how hard that must've been for her.'

He felt her turn towards him, but he kept his eyes on the road.

'It must've been hard for you too, Harry.'

'It was the worst time of my life,' he found himself admitting. She'd just been so open with him. It felt wrong not to be equally open.

He parked outside her workshop, but neither

of them made a move to get out. He knew she wouldn't ask him in. He tried telling himself he was glad about that.

'I thought we were going to lose her.' His heart clenched, as he remembered the darkness of that time.

'But she pulled through.' That quiet voice pulled him back from the abyss. 'You helped her do that. Your strength and your patience, she told me it made all the difference.'

He turned to stare. When had she told her that? It must've been when he'd popped to the cellar for another bottle of wine. 'I didn't do anything—just held her hand, nagged her to not give up, to keep going…to keep fighting.'

'You were there when she needed you. She knows you're one person she can always rely on. Don't downplay it. It's a big thing. She worships you, you know?'

He met her gaze in the dim light of the car's interior. 'She means a lot to me too. I'm still angry that my parents weren't there for her. That they were too caught up in their own mess to see what was happening.'

She frowned. 'I know you said your father headed for the hills, but surely for something as important as this…?'

'I contacted him.' He hadn't wanted to. He hadn't forgiven him for tearing their family apart, but he'd have done anything to help Lily. 'You know what he said? He said Lily wasn't his flesh and blood and, therefore, no concern of his.'

Her hand flew to her mouth, horror reflected in her eyes. He nodded. 'Charming, right?'

'I can't…there aren't even words for that.'

There were, but she was too polite to utter them. 'About the only good thing to come from Lily's illness is it shook my mother out of her self-indulgent martyrdom. She raced home and organised the best treatment possible, sat with Lily almost as much as I did.'

'So…she *was* there for Lily.'

'Eventually. But it took the shock of Lily nearly dying to make her realise what was important!' He dragged both hands through his hair. 'To make her remember she still had children who were relying on her.'

'Oh, Harry, I'm sorry.'

'Don't waste your sympathy on me, Ella. I was fine. During all of the ugliness of the divorce I still had my skiing to focus on.' He'd been making a splash on the junior circuit by then. 'But Lily…' The old guilt and anger rose through him. 'She must've felt abandoned by us all. She'd already lost one set of parents to a car accident—'

'None of it was your fault, Harry.' She seized his hand, shook it until he looked at her. 'None of it! You were a child yourself.'

She was wrong. He should've seen what was happening with Lily.

'It's in the past now. Lily has become a lovely, vibrant young woman who wants to make her mark on the world. She got through it. You all got through it.'

A breath eased out of him, and he nodded. He was determined that nothing would ever upset Lily's equilibrium like that again. He squeezed Ella's hand and then released it. In the stillness and the darkness his physical awareness for her grew, and he needed to keep it in check.

'It's why sealing this deal with Bright Directions is so important. And why I'm determined to never make the same mistakes my father made.' Rock hard resolution settled in his chest. 'It's why I'll never become involved with any woman long term.'

She shook her head. 'Bzzz.' She made the sound of a game-show buzzer and raised her hand. 'I'll have to stop you there, Mr Gillespie, and ask you to explain. I don't see how that second statement follows the first.'

He hauled in a breath. 'I know it's not fair to blame my father for Lily's eating disorder, but he let her down—badly. She thought he loved her, she trusted him, and she blamed herself when he turned his back on her, blamed herself for the divorce. She said her coming into the family unit created the extra stress that broke my parents' marriage.'

Ella's eyes shimmered with sympathy. 'Poor Lily,' she whispered.

'The thing is, I knew about my father's infidelity. I confronted him about it when I was thirteen.' A year before the divorce. 'He told me he felt suffocated—that the only way he could remain married to my mother was by having extramarital affairs. He said as long as my mother never found out about them, they couldn't hurt her. He said that as long as we maintained the status quo, our family would survive.'

'Of all the—'

She broke off, but even in the darkness of the car he could see the way her eyes flashed.

'He emotionally blackmailed you into keeping his secret!'

And he had kept the secret. Not that it had made any difference. Not in the end. His father's lies had torn their family apart.

'Harry, you have to see that wasn't fair. And it doesn't make you like your father. You were only thirteen!'

'I saw what his betrayal did to my mother and Lily. I'm never doing that to a woman. *Ever.* I refuse to be responsible for hurting someone so badly.'

'Harry, you're *not* your father.'

'I loathe my father, Ella.' Acid burned his throat. 'But apparently I'm my father's son. That sense of suffocation he described to me?' He turned and met her gaze. 'I feel it too. As soon as a woman becomes too clingy, it's like I can't breathe and am going to die a slow and horrible death.'

She stared at him with wide horrified eyes. She'd started to shake her head, but broke off, her fingers going to her throat.

'What's worse—' he forced himself to continue '—when I feel like that, I don't blame him for running.'

She pressed a hand to her mouth. Those blue eyes filling with tears. 'Oh, Harry.'

His jaw ached he clenched it so hard. So did his hands. 'I won't make the same mistake he did. I won't mislead any woman into thinking I can offer her anything lasting or substantial. Some people are made for the long haul, and some aren't. I'm not, and I refuse to pretend otherwise.'

CHAPTER SEVEN

'The party's *here*?'

Ella did her best to not look too awed when they pulled up outside of one of Sydney's most elite venues.

'Stop fidgeting,' Harry said when she touched nervous fingers to the gathered straps of her sleeveless gown. 'You look great.'

'You haven't even seen me properly yet.'

He'd sent a driver to collect her *in a limousine no less* before it fetched him from his Woolloomooloo town house.

'I'm sorry. I got held up at the office and—'

'Harry, you're doing me a favour. Don't apologise.' She peered out of the window. 'I'm nervous, that's all. What if I get in there and become star-struck and stupid?' That wouldn't impress the trustees of his charity.

'Celebrities are just people too.'

She snorted.

'You weren't star-struck by me.'

'No, but…' She'd had a lot on her mind the

night they'd met. She'd barely given his fame and celebrity a thought. It was his humour and empathy that had made an impact.

'We're making a deal—we're sticking close to each other tonight, okay? I'll save you from any star-struck moments, and you'll save me from any scary women. Deal?'

'Deal.'

He reached out and squeezed her hand. 'Ready?'

'Ready.'

'Wow!' he breathed when he handed her out.

He stared at her with the strangest expression and her stomach dropped. She glanced down, praying she hadn't somehow stained the fine satin of her dress.

'You look like a film starlet from the...'

'Nineteen-forties.' She wore a nineteen-forties-inspired evening dress in pale blue satin.

'You look *amazing.*'

She glanced back up and her heart started to gallop. He looked as if he wanted to *devour her.*

In that moment she was perilously close to offering herself up as a five-course banquet. Speaking of delectable things, Harry's crisp white shirt and bow tie made him look like a prince while his waistcoat hugged his powerful form in a way that—

Don't!

She couldn't let this go to her head. Flirting came as naturally to Harry as breathing. She forced herself into speech. 'When you said it was black tie, I thought this would be suitable.'

'This is one of yours? You *made* it?'

He continued to survey her with far too much male appreciation. 'I, um…don't own any floor-length gowns that I haven't made myself.'

She skimmed her hands along the gathered hipline and ordered herself not to babble about the five outside radiating darts—he wasn't interested in any of that. 'It is okay, isn't it? You don't mind that I'm wearing one of my own designs?' Had she inadvertently made a faux pas?

'It's perfect.'

But the smile he sent her was tight and she couldn't help feeling she'd got something wrong. Unless…

Dear God. Had he seen the effect he'd had on her? Was he starting to feel the jaws of that awful suffocation he'd described closing around him? The thought that *she* could make him feel like that…

She pressed her hands to her stomach. She couldn't think of anything worse!

She entered the ballroom on autopilot, her mind weaving in drunken circles as she searched for ways to put his mind at rest, but then he started pointing people out to her, explaining who was connected to whom, the deals going down and the latest celebrity gossip, becoming as warm and easy as ever again, and she was able to let out a sigh of relief.

The event was pure over-the-top glamour. Women she'd only ever seen in the society pages strutted beneath gleaming chandeliers in gowns that dazzled. Wait staff in spotless white uniforms circulated platters of oysters. Tables laden with the most sumptuous delicacies stood at one end of the room, while at the other a five-piece orchestra crooned swoony music. A glass of champagne was placed in her hand and she and Harry made a slow circuit of the room. She met the trustees of Bright Directions and their partners, and it all seemed ridiculously convivial. Wait until she told everyone about this tomorrow!

The moment Harry absented himself to procure her a plate of food, she found one of the trustees at her elbow. Donald was a former politician and she doubted the timing was an accident. 'Are you enjoying yourself?' he asked, introducing his wife, Rita.

'I'm having a lovely time. It's such a treat to be here.' She leaned in close to whisper. 'I feel as if I've stepped into another world.'

They both laughed. 'You look a vision yourself,' Rita said. 'Your gown is divine.'

'While we men are desperately jealous of Harrison's waistcoat.'

It was her turn to laugh. 'It suits him, doesn't it?' Tiny mountains were picked out in silver thread on a midnight dark background. There was no denying he looked fabulous in it.

'He's inordinately proud of it. And your gown. He's been handing out your business card to all and sundry.'

He was doing *what*? 'Good Lord, where did he get those from?' She pressed a hand to her waist when Rita pulled one from her purse. 'They're old. I'm having them redesigned—'

The older woman patted her arm. 'As long as the contact details are correct, nobody will care what your card looks like.' She popped it back into her purse. 'What the two of you are wearing is advertisement enough.'

'That's very kind of you,' she managed, touched that Harry was going to so much trouble for her.

'My dear,' Donald started, 'please don't take this the wrong way, but I'm surprised to find a woman like you on Harry's arm.'

'Donald!'

Rita sent him a scandalised glare, but Ella only laughed. 'You mean an old-fashioned girl like me?'

She straightened. Maybe she could repay Harry all his kindness.

'You shouldn't believe everything you read in the papers. Harry's not a saint and I'm not saying he is, but he's not the playboy he's made out to be either.'

'Are you and he…?'

'We're very good friends,' she told him firmly.

She stared from Donald to Rita and made a sudden decision. 'Harry has been helping me through a rather difficult time. Eighteen months ago my fiancé died in a terrible accident. Harry has helped me turn my face towards the future. He's made me realise it's the only positive thing to do, that anything else would be a sad homage to pay to a man I loved.'

And she had loved James. Dearly.

'Oh, my dear.'

Rita's eyes grew suspiciously bright and Ella waved a finger at her. 'Don't you start or you'll set me off. Obviously what I just told you isn't something I publicise, but I know what Harry's trying to achieve by going into partnership with you.'

Donald blinked.

'I think someone with Harry's empathy and enthusiasm is a perfect fit for your charity.'

Donald's gaze sharpened and she saw the shrewdness that had made him such a successful politician. She held his gaze. She had nothing to hide. She'd meant every word.

Slowly the older man nodded. 'It was the conclusion I was coming to myself, but it's nice to have it confirmed. And speak of the devil…'

She turned to find Harry approaching. She spread her hands. 'Where's my promised delicious delicacies?'

'Australia's leading starlet intercepted me on

the way over here and said, "It's simply too good
of you, darling," and whisked the plate from my
hand.'

They all laughed.

Those whisky warm eyes rested on her. 'Would
you like to dance instead?'

'One dance,' she told him, working hard to keep
her voice light, refusing to dwell on how she'd
manage to maintain her equilibrium in his arms.
'And then I'll be venturing forth to find my own
food.'

'Before you go—' Donald clapped Harry on the
shoulder '—I'm convinced we could do something
special together, Harry.'

Harry straightened. 'So am I.'

'Can you meet with me first thing Monday?'

'Absolutely.'

'Bring your lawyers and let's see what we can
thrash out. I'll look forward to talking more.'

The older couple ambled off and Harry swung
to her. 'What did you do?'

She tried to rein in her grin, but couldn't. 'Oh,
you know… Promised him half a dozen waistcoats and threw in an evening gown for his wife.
Just common run-of-the-mill bribery.'

His jaw dropped.

'Joking,' she said, taking his arm and leading
him towards the dance floor, and away from a fa-
mous pop singer who'd started to bear down on

them with a determined glint in her eyes. 'Scary lady at nine o'clock.'

He immediately took her in his arms and she found herself enfolded in his scent and his heat. Being pressed against the long lean length of him fired every cell in her body to aching life.

'Tell me what you said to Donald.'

His breath disturbed the hair at her temple, sending a curl brushing against her ear. An electric thrill arrowed straight to her nipples. She could feel them harden and press against the satin of her dress. If anyone was looking... She swallowed. She was never wearing satin near Harry again!

'Ella?'

She had to swallow before she could speak. 'I told him his organisation should be proud to associate themselves with a man like you.'

He eased back, raised an eyebrow.

'Someone with your compassion and enthusiasm.'

His mouth fell open. Firm sculpted lips and—

She forced her gaze over his left shoulder, did what she could to ignore the yearning that swamped her. 'I told him you were the kind of person who helped others find joy in life again.'

His hand tightened about hers and she glanced back up. And found herself in imminent danger of falling into the depths of his eyes.

Would it matter if she did?

The thought slid beneath her guard, making her heart hammer. *Would* it matter? She'd been celibate for eighteen months. She was young and healthy…and sex for fun was something she could really get behind at the moment.

Her body hummed its approval. She sensed that making love with Harry would be exhilarating, extraordinary. And so, *so* satisfying.

Stop! He's trying to clean up his image. After everything he's done to help you, you want to repay him like that?

She dragged her gaze away, moved back until she could feel air between them again, ruthlessly ignoring her body's protest. 'I merely confirmed his own opinion, so it's nothing. And I think we're being watched so we'd better be on our best behaviour for the rest of the evening.'

She glanced up to find a puzzled smile on his lips. 'It's not *nothing*. You're amazing, you know that?'

'Don't be silly.'

'I knew bringing you tonight was a good idea. I just hadn't realised how good. I'm very grateful, Ella, and—'

'Me too.' She sent him a tight smile and tried to temper her curtness. In less than thirty seconds the song would end and she'd be able to breathe again. 'Besides, quid pro quo and all that. You scratch my back and I'll scratch yours.'

Don't think about fingernails and naked backs.

'I heard what you've been doing,' she added. If she kept talking maybe it would help her keep everything else in check. 'Handing out my business card.'

He blinked and frowned.

'If we stay on the straight and narrow, we'll both get what we want.' The song ended and she promptly moved out of his arms. 'Excellent.' She'd managed to not ravish him on the dance floor. 'Let's go get some food.'

Neither she nor Harry had wanted a late night—they were holding their pseudo hen and stag parties tomorrow—so they made a strategic retreat at midnight. He insisted on seeing her home, and they were literally only around the corner from the venue, when he swung to her. 'What did I do wrong?'

'What do you mean? You didn't do anything wrong.' She frowned. Had she missed something? 'Donald and Rita said goodnight to us very warmly. I don't think—'

'Not with them, with you. What did I do wrong with you?'

Her heart started to thump. 'I've no idea what you're talking about.'

He slid the privacy screen up between them and the driver. 'On the dance floor…something happened. You changed.'

It took her last reserve of strength to not press

cool hands to burning cheeks. All evening she'd thought she'd hidden her emotions, but she hadn't fooled him for a moment. 'Harry, I promise. You did nothing wrong.'

'Was it Donald and Rita, then? Did they say something to upset you or—?'

'No!' She couldn't let him think that. She dragged in a deep breath. 'Will you please just let the subject drop?'

'No.'

She closed her eyes.

'Ella, we're friends. Will you please tell me what's wrong?'

Ella turned positively green and Harry's stomach lurched. 'Are you ill?' Did she need to see a doctor?

She shook her head, turning to stare out of the window. 'Adults,' he heard her murmur. 'We're adults.' As if she was giving herself a pep talk.

Before he could ponder that further, she squared her shoulders and turned back. 'It's not you, Harry. It's me.'

His brows wanted to shoot up towards his hairline, but with a superhuman effort he forced them not to. When her eyes narrowed, though, he realised his brows now lowered in a frown. He did what he could to smooth his face out. 'This sounds ominously like a break-up speech.'

'We're not a couple so we can't be breaking up.'

'You can break a friendship up.' It hit him then that he didn't want her breaking their friendship up. He enjoyed spending time with her. She made him laugh. When he was around her he could relax…be himself.

'This isn't a break-up speech. I'm not trying to break anything up.' Her gaze slid away. 'Look, let's just drop this and—'

'Not a chance.' He sat up straighter, aching to fix whatever was wrong. She'd had enough to deal with for the last eighteen months. She could abdicate responsibility to him.

She barely moved a muscle, and yet he could've sworn she wanted to drop her head to her hands. She didn't. Instead she lifted her chin in his direction, but her gaze didn't meet his. 'This hardly needs saying, Harry, but you're a very attractive man.'

He hated how tense she'd become. 'Are you sure this isn't a break-up speech?' he teased. 'It's sounding more and more like one.'

The corners of her mouth twitched, just for a moment. 'Can't you be serious for ten minutes?'

Sure he could, when he had to be. But he really wanted to hear her laugh.

Her mouth pressed into a firm line. 'No falling in love. No breaking up.'

'That's my motto.'

'Except I've been celibate for eighteen months, and…'

He couldn't begin to imagine it. 'And?'

She grimaced. 'And in those eighteen months the closest I've been to a man who isn't related to me was this evening on the dance floor with you.'

Her meaning hit him then. He rocked back in his seat.

'See?' she hissed, clearly misinterpreting his reaction as shock, rather than what it truly was—excitement. 'So when I said it wasn't you, that you did nothing wrong, I meant it. It was me—all me. And this would've been better left unsaid. It would've saved us a lot of embarrassment.'

'Ella—'

'Look, I know it's normal, all right? So, please, no platitudes.'

Platitudes were the last thing on his mind.

'And I get that I should find it…*unsettling*. But you want to know what I find really confronting? You invited me to the party tonight out of kindness.' Her bottom lip wobbled. 'And maybe pity.'

He stabbed a finger to the leather car seat between them. 'Not pity.'

'But you did it to introduce me to influential people and help get my name out there. You didn't have to do that.'

'I did it because I believe in you.'

'See?' She lifted her hands as if he'd said something dreadful. 'You're this great guy who's trying to do meaningful things with a seriously worthy charity, and I promised to act as a kind of shield tonight because I knew how important it was for you to present a wholesome image. But little did I know you'd need a shield against me!' She met his gaze. 'But when we were out on the dance floor, Harry, I didn't care about any of that. All I could think about was what it'd be like to get naked with you and—'

He pressed his fingers to her lips. 'Not helping,' he ground out, trying to get the thundering of his blood under control.

She stared at him and her eyes widened as they raked his face. 'No,' she whispered.

But it sounded less like a refutation than a revelation.

'No,' she said again, shaking her head. 'I'm not the kind of woman you'd find attractive.'

He blinked. 'What kind of woman would that be?'

'Beautiful.'

Dear God. This woman.

He undid his seat belt, slid across to the middle seat and put that seat belt on instead.

Her eyes went wide. 'What are you doing?'

'You are beautiful, Elle.'

'Don't be ridiculous.' Her throat bobbed. 'And what did you just call me?'

'Did you not look at yourself in the mirror tonight?'

The limousine was roomy, but this close they couldn't help but brush thighs and arms. And every touch fired a shot of energy and desire through his blood. He knew it did for her too from the way she tried to shift away to avoid—how had she phrased it?—feeling unsettled by the rush of feelings they evoked in each other. The rocking of the car, though, made it impossible, and he had no desire, or intention, of avoiding it.

He wanted to touch all of her. He wanted to explore her every inch with his hands and mouth. He craved to know what would give her pleasure, and he hungered to feel those small clever hands on his body—

He hauled himself back, appalled at how consumed he'd become by the fantasy he'd started to weave. They had a couple of things to clear up first. 'You are beautiful,' he repeated, 'but, like every other woman on the planet, you're going to say, *Oh, but this part of me is too big, and this part is too small, while that bit is too wide, and there's a blemish there...* Yada-yada-yada.'

'"Yada" being a technical term, I suppose?' But her breath hitched as she said it and he knew her equilibrium was hanging by a thread. Just like his.

'You *are* beautiful, Ella, but you also have an inner fire that lights you up from the inside out, and it's drawing me like a proverbial moth.' He wanted to dive right down into the middle of that flame.

Playing with fire is dangerous.

He shook the thought off. He was adept at not

getting burned and making sure nobody else got burned either.

She stared at him as if she hadn't properly seen him until this very minute.

'I really want to kiss you,' he said, his heart thumping with need. 'I've wanted to kiss you since I first saw you in the restaurant when you barely registered who I was.'

Her chin shot up. 'I registered!'

'Can I kiss you, Elle?'

She swallowed. 'God, when you call me that...' Desire-drenched eyes met his. 'I want you to kiss me so badly, I think I might die if you don't.'

As they spoke, they turned more fully to each other. He cupped her face, revelling in the softness of her skin and the fine bones beneath his fingertips. Her fingers closed about his lapels and they pulled each other closer as if they each had a magnet drawing the other nearer and nearer. Millimetres from each other's lips, they paused—as if to breathe each other in, as if fixing the moment in their minds—and then their mouths came together and there was nothing tentative about that.

For a brief moment he felt unbalanced, as if he'd hit ice on his skis and was in danger of crashing down a mountain, but at the last moment Ella's mouth opened beneath his and everything suddenly righted itself.

He couldn't put together a single coherent thought after that. Sensation pounded through him—glorious, exhilarating and better than any damn race he'd ever run. Ella's mouthed moved against his, just as hungry, just as demanding, driving him to new heights, filling him with a wild, desperate need.

Lips, teeth, tongue—all teasing inevitable rhythm. Her hands on his jaw, fingernails scraping lightly across the designer stubble he swore he wore for just this purpose. But it had never felt this good before. Small strong hands that moved from the sides of his neck to splay across his chest, pushing aside his waistcoat, to glory in his heat and the muscled strength of his torso.

Dear God, it wasn't nearly enough. He needed more. Where the hell was the zip on her dress?

He found it—a side zip—and lowered it, before bringing his fingers back up, knuckles brushing against the side of her breast. He caught her shocked cry in his mouth, and the electric ripple of her body flowed through him too. Pressing kisses to her throat, he lowered the bodice of her dress until her breasts were proudly exposed in the sheerest of white lace bras.

He brushed his knuckles down the sides of both breasts and again that shocked gasp and electric shudder ripped through her. Leaning forward, he drew one erect nipple into his mouth and laved it with his tongue. She arched into him, her hands partially lifted as if to tunnel into his hair, but her arms stopped short, pinned to her sides by the bodice of her dress, and a primal roar of satisfaction filled him.

When she was lying half reclined like that, lips kiss-swollen, hair mussed and her breasts exposed for his delectation as she gazed up at him, eyes drunk with arousal, he felt like a king or sultan. And every time he ran the backs of his fingers along the sides of her breast, another electric jolt shook her.

Her nipples grew harder and tighter. He drew her other nipple into his mouth, and continued the knuckle brushing down the sides of her breasts until she was sobbing with need. Could he make her come just from this? He'd love to try and—

'Harry.'

Her voice, threaded with need, drew him back and he suddenly froze. Was he really in danger of taking her in the back of his car like some randy teenager? She hadn't made love to a man in eighteen months. *Eighteen months!*

She deserved to be wooed and cherished... made to feel like a queen. She deserved fine champagne, a king-size bed, and Egyptian cotton sheets. She deserved a man who would make the experience memorable.

He dragged in a breath before lifting his head. 'Spend the night with me, Ella.' He'd take her back to his place and give her everything she wanted—and everything she didn't know she wanted. He'd shower her with so much attention it'd turn her head.

She stared into his eyes and he saw the desire, the yearning, the temptation all reflected there. She wanted him every bit as much as he wanted her.

And then she closed her eyes, her face screwing up tight. 'We can't, Harry. Oh, God, we can't.'

Every muscle screamed a protest. He wanted to argue. He wanted to kiss her until she stopped thinking and started feeling again...until she begged him not to stop.

Instead, he pulled the bodice of her dress back up, and slid back into his original seat to try and give them both the air they desperately needed, averting his gaze as she drew up her zipper and tried to straighten herself back out again.

'Why can't we?' he asked when he was sure he could control his voice and ask the question gently. She didn't deserve his frustration. She deserved his understanding.

She remained silent for so long he didn't think she was going to answer. 'I won't do anything that could cast a shadow over Susie's wedding,' she finally said. 'It wouldn't be fair.'

He opened his mouth.

'I know you don't think it's fair that the family has any say in my sex life.'

'You don't *have* a sex life, Ella.' And she wasn't

likely to get one if she continued to let her family have any say in the matter.

'When I do start dating again it's going to cause a ruckus. I'll deal with that as and when I have to, but the lead up to Susie's wedding definitely isn't the time.'

He dragged a hand down his face. She had a point. Had he completely forgotten his promise to Martin? He had a duty as best man to ensure the wedding ran as smoothly as it could.

'And anyway—'

He could feel the heat of her gaze.

'What happened to your no romance rule? I know you don't want to do anything to jeopardise your deal with Bright Directions. Why risk that for a quick fling with me?'

Ice stepped down his spine and slowly but inexorably filled his chest, spreading out to his limbs until they felt like frozen lead. The charity deal was so important to Lily, meant so much to her. Was he really so selfish that he'd endanger it?

His lips thinned. He was exactly like his father. He'd been fighting it all his life, but what further proof did he need? And that meant he had to stay away from a woman like Ella. 'You're right. I'm sorry. I lost my head.'

'I'm sorry too.'

He had to close his eyes against the need that threaded her whisper.

They barely spoke again until the car pulled

up in front of her workshop. He slid out first and offered her his hand, but she ignored it. He didn't blame her. Touch was a torment. He didn't offer to walk her to her door. 'I'll wait here until you're inside.'

She glanced up. 'I'm—'

'I'll see you Sunday,' he cut in. 'Good luck tomorrow. I hope the day is a roaring success. We'll compare notes on Sunday.'

She dragged in a breath and nodded. 'Goodnight, Harry.'

CHAPTER EIGHT

WHEN HARRY'S CAR pulled up outside her workshop on Sunday morning, Ella didn't bother pretending that she hadn't noticed. She stood in the doorway as he strode towards her, those long legs covering the distance with a loose-limbed ease that had all the feelings he'd evoked in her on Friday night roaring to instant life.

Don't think about Friday night.

Of course, she hadn't been able to think of anything else since.

Then think of Susie.

That, at least, had her pushing her shoulders back and pasting on a smile. One glance into his face, though, had her gaze sliding away. 'C'mon in, it's turned chilly.'

This time Tuesday they'd be on a plane winging their way to the balmy climes of Malaysia, leaving the winter chill behind. *It'll be fun.* She gritted her teeth and tried harder. *It'll be fun!*

'Did you want another sewing lesson while we

compare notes about yesterday's events?' Yesterday had been their unofficial hen and stag parties.

'Love one.'

She'd put an inordinate amount of thought into this meeting, hadn't wanted them to sit awkwardly at the table, staring at each other while nursing mugs of coffee. It'd be easier to talk if they had something else to focus on.

She moved to the sewing machines. 'You've mastered the main construction of the boxy tops I make for the markets.'

The tops were ridiculously easy to make—nothing more than a back and front, sewn together, with simple cuff sleeves. But she made them in such breezy bright fabrics that they flew off the racks. Inexpensive to make, and she priced them to sell.

'Those sleeves were tricky.' He took a seat at what had become *his* machine.

'But you got the hang of them.' He'd insisted on unpicking one sleeve three times to get it perfect. His determination had impressed her. 'There're just two more things to do before your top is finished.'

He swung to her. 'No way!'

'Yes way. And the first of those is to bias bind the neckline.' She pointed. 'The bias binding is the long thin piece we cut.'

She'd set his work in progress beside his workstation and grabbed a finished top from the pile she was working on. 'This is what we want our finished product to look like.'

He took it and studied the neckline thoroughly. She swallowed at the intensity of his gaze. Dear God. If she'd said yes to spending the night with him on Friday evening, all of that amazing focus would've been squarely concentrated on her and—

She rattled back into speech. 'This is how we attach it.' She showed him how to pin the binding to the neckline. 'And we sew along there.'

'Fiddly,' he muttered.

That was the plan—to keep his attention focussed elsewhere rather than on her. 'The sleeves were fiddly too, but you managed those. Just take it slow. Cuppa?'

'Maybe later.'

Damn. She'd hoped for a break from the enticing scent of leather and amber. Seizing one of the unfinished tops from her pile, she started sewing. She'd attached bias binding to necklines so often she could do it on autopilot. Gritting her teeth, she did exactly that now.

'You are demoralisingly fast.'

She glanced across to find him staring at her with a frown in his eyes. She straightened. Did he think she was showing off? 'Oh, Harry, I've done this so many times I could do it with my eyes closed. Not recommended, of course. Needles are sharp. You don't want one going into a finger.'

He leaned fractionally closer. 'You've done that?'

'Only the once.'

That made him laugh and the laugh lightened something inside her. She gestured at her sewing machine. 'The equivalent would be if you put me on a pair of skis. I've never skied in my life, and I promise you don't want to see that. I'd spend more time flat on my face than upright.'

'You're wrong. I would like to see that.'

'Ha! So you could get a few cheap laughs.'

The colour in his eyes became richer and deeper. 'So I could watch you master the necessary skills,' he corrected. 'I think you'd love it. There's nothing like the freedom of flying down a mountain, the air crisp and cold, the sky blue and everything dazzling white and sparkling like crystal.'

She almost said, 'When can we go?' She gulped the words back. 'How did the boys' day go yesterday?'

He was quiet for a moment, but when she glanced at him, he'd turned back to his machine. 'It was great, really relaxed.'

'Even the dads?'

He nodded and she let out a breath she hadn't known she'd been holding. It occurred to her in that moment how grateful she was to him. For *so* many things.

'After the baseball—which was a real hit, by

the way—it was back to mine for burgers and beer and games of pool. It wasn't a particularly late night, but it was nice to kick back.'

'Sounds perfect.'

'Your turn.'

She gave up all pretence of sewing. 'It was mixed. The fittings were fun. Everyone loves their outfits. And as you suggested, I played the soundtracks from *Grease*, *Mamma Mia* and *Dirty Dancing* while we did that. The mums were in good form and we all hummed and swayed along in good moods. Susie couldn't stop smiling.'

'So why aren't *you* smiling now?'

She moistened her lips. 'I hadn't realised our picture made the society pages.'

He grimaced. 'Ah.'

'And neither did the mums or Susie. However, Cousin Adele…remember her?'

'The tragic one?'

She nodded. 'When the larger party arrived, she took a lot of glee in showing said society page around.' She'd had to endure a series of pointed questions. 'I told them it was a work thing.' Which was exactly what it had been.

'Did they believe you?'

'I think so, but Auntie Rachel was quiet for the rest of the day.' Which meant her mum had been quiet too.

She'd organised a painting party. A café in the city held social painting evenings, and it had become all the rage. She'd spoken to the artist who ran the events and she'd agreed to run a private party for them. Set up with easels, canvases and paints, they'd endeavoured to paint Susie in a silly mock veil. Susie had loved it.

The mums had said they'd had fun, but that hadn't stopped them casting perturbed glances in her direction whenever they thought she wasn't looking. They'd felt betrayed. She'd seen it in their eyes. Not only had she left the family firm, but she'd also gone on a date with a man who wasn't James. And even if that date had been platonic, it was still a milestone. Another infinitesimal shift away from James.

'They need to get used to the idea of you moving on, Ella.'

His words pulled her back. 'Yes, but not the week of the wedding.'

'Not this week.' His mouth tightened and he turned back to his sewing machine. But his words didn't sound like agreement. They sounded like a warning. 'Not this week,' he repeated as if to wedge them in his mind.

Her eyes narrowed. If she didn't know better, she'd think he was up to something.

He straightened. 'Did I tell you I spoke to the resort manager? He's making sure everything we requested is on hand.'

'Excellent.' They'd come up with a range of group activities to keep things light and fun for the week, to help everyone get into the holiday spirit; to give Susie and Martin a week they could look back on with pride for the rest of their lives. Ella crossed her fingers.

'What now?'

She snapped to. What did he mean?

He held the top towards her and she realised he was referring to the sewing.

She scrutinised his stitches. 'What are you? Some child sewing prodigy?' She handed it back. 'That's amazingly neat.'

'I'm hardly a child, Ella.'

His lips twisted, and every moment of Friday night with her dress down around her waist and his hands and lips on her breasts rose up between them. She tried to drag her gaze from his, but he held it captive.

'This isn't working,' he bit out, gesturing at the sewing machines.

She didn't bother misunderstanding him. 'Well, I don't imagine talking about it is going to help either, so if you have any other bright ideas, I'm all ears.'

'Oh, I'm full of bright ideas.' He slid across on the castor wheels of his chair, closing the distance between them with a speed that had her gulping. His hands went either side of her on the table, his bulk and his heat crowding her in. 'Here's one— we race upstairs right now, make mad passionate love until we've had our fill and get this thing out of our system.'

Had she ever been more tempted by anything in her life?

'Just say the word, Ella, and I'm there. Or if you don't want to speak, just nod.'

Her heart tried to hammer a path right out of her chest. She couldn't think when he was this close. Planting a hand on that broad, hard chest, she gently pushed. He gave way immediately. 'There are too many flaws with that plan.'

He folded his arms. 'Hit me with them.'

'They'll know.' The mums would know.

He looked suddenly tired. 'Ella…'

She thought her heart would break at the expression in his eyes. 'I know! I know!' The family had no right to judge her. She had nothing to feel guilty about. 'But I won't do anything that could cast a shadow on Susie's wedding. She lost a brother she dearly loved, Harry. This is a new beginning for her and I don't want anything to mar it.'

'And when do you get your new beginning?'

She gestured at her workshop. 'I'm making a start.'

He dragged a hand down his face. 'What other flaws are there in my plan?' he eventually asked, pointing upstairs as if to remind her of the plan.

As if she could forget it! She swallowed. 'I don't

think once is going to be enough to get this thing out of my system, Harry.'

He shot out of his chair and raced around the drafting table until its bulk stood between him and her. He braced his arms against it as if to stop from…what? Hauling her into his arms and kissing her?

Her pulse went mad.

'Eighteen months is a long time to…' Today it felt like an eternity. 'And I don't want to start something now that's in danger of spiralling out of control for the next week and—' She broke off, refusing to let her mind dwell on tropical beaches and balmy, starlit nights. 'My focus needs to stay centred on the wedding.'

She risked glancing across at him. Both his hands and eyes were clenched and he was dragging in deep breaths as if he was counting. She wanted to yell at him to find someone else to torment if he was feeling all hot and bothered, but the thought of him with another woman…

She flinched.

He pointed a finger at her. 'As soon as we're back in Australia, you and I are going out on the town, Ella. I'm going to wine and dine you and shower you with attention and spoil you. At the end of the evening I'm going to do my utmost to seduce you. And I'm going to do it again and again until you've had your fill.'

Best plan ever! She wanted that so badly, but…

Don't be an idiot.

She made herself laugh. 'We're from such totally different worlds, Harry. You're a successful high-flying millionaire and former world champion while I'm a nobody who barely has two brass tacks to rub together at the moment. We run in different circles.' She rested an elbow on the table and brow in her hand. 'I've absolutely no expectation of seeing you again once we return to Australia.'

The words tasted bitter in her mouth, but she forced herself to say them, forced herself to face the reality. It was better to face that reality now than later. 'No expectations at all,' she repeated.

Harry froze at Ella's words. Very slowly he straightened. 'You really believe that?'

She lifted her head and it looked as if it took all of her energy to do so. Lines of exhaustion fanned out from her eyes, but he hardened his heart. 'If that's what you think friendship means to me then you're right, we've nothing else to talk about.'

He shoved his arms into the coat he'd shrugged off when he'd arrived. 'I'm glad to have found this out now, though, rather than a week or two down the line, because I make it a rule to not sleep with women who have such a low opinion of me.'

She shot to her feet. 'Oh, Harry, wait. I—'

But he'd already started for the door. A white-hot anger he'd not experienced since he was a kid had him in its grip and he knew he had to get out of here before he unleashed its full force on her.

Had anyone ever offended him quite so fully? Had he ever felt more disappointed in his life? How had he got her so wrong?

He sensed what he was feeling was out of proportion to the crime, but he couldn't think straight.

Before he lashed out, he needed to think straight.

'Harry, I—'

He swung around. 'Once we return from Malaysia, I expect you'll have no trouble whatsoever finding someone to help you scratch whatever itch you need scratching. For as long as it needs scratching.'

She paled and took a step back.

He stalked out of the door and didn't look back.

Harry did everything to avoid Ella at the airport on Tuesday. He'd taken her call yesterday, but only because he'd thought it might have something to do with the wedding. When she'd tried to stutter out an apology, he'd cut her off with a curt, 'Not now, Ella,' and had hung up.

She'd evidently got the message, because other than a nod and quiet, 'Hello, Harry,' in the airport lounge, she'd kept her distance.

Which was exactly what he wanted!

But he was now crammed into a window seat beside second cousin once-removed Uncle Aubrey, while Ella was hemmed in in a middle row with the great-aunts.

The wedding group were all roughly seated in the same section but scattered about in pockets. The benefit of that meant there was plenty of seat-hopping. The downside was that Adele— the tragic one—kept casting glances in his direction. With Ella no longer running interference for him, he knew the moment Aubrey vacated his seat Adele would fill it.

Harry did everything he could to avoid the Adeles of the world. She was the kind of woman who'd claim she only wanted a bit of fun, but that clearly wasn't the case. She'd want everything—love, marriage, babies. It wouldn't matter how often he said he wasn't interested in any of that, she'd be certain she could change his mind.

All hell would break loose when she realised he was in earnest. There'd be scenes. He'd be accused of misleading her, of taking advantage. Sweat broke out on his top lip. He'd promised Martin he'd keep things running smoothly. He couldn't afford that kind of scene.

Serves you right for not accepting Ella's apology.

If only he could catch Ella's eye… But he was pressed up hard in his window seat while she was in that darn middle row, several rows ahead of him. He could see her dark curls from time to time. He fancied that they drooped rather than bounced, and he cursed silently.

Why the hell had he taken such offence on Sunday anyway? If the papers were anything to go by, he was a fly-by-night who didn't have a serious bone in his body. Why should she trust him? What true signs of friendship had he actually given her?

He'd offered her business his support. And then he'd pressured her for sex! He'd told her he was off dating and romance, and yet he'd kissed her and asked her to spend the night with him. Why *would* she trust him?

As if his imagination had conjured her, she walked past on her way to the restrooms. She didn't spare him a single glance. He didn't blame her. He cursed himself for not thinking quicker and finding a way to make her stop and talk to him and Aubrey.

Aubrey broke off his monologue about the three months he'd spent in India forty years ago—a reminiscence that thankfully required very little input from Harry—to say, 'I hope you're not thinking of messing with our Ellie.'

He wanted to tell the other man to go to hell. The savage urge made him blink. Alpha confrontations and testosterone-driven beatings of his chest had never been his style. It made too many ugly headlines. Humour and charm had always been his weapons of choice.

'I like Ella a lot. And I respect her. We're

friends. I can't imagine anyone here having a problem with that, can you?'

'I guess not.' But the older man looked dubious, and in that moment Harry realised the seating arrangement hadn't been a happy accident. It had been managed by the family.

He shuffled upright. *Game on.*

He nodded towards the great-aunts. 'I believe Edith has been trying to catch your eye.' He paused. 'She's a fine-looking woman, don't you think?'

'I… Well…' Aubrey straightened and squared his shoulders. 'She has an admirable sense of style.'

'If you want a tip from me, and I have quite the reputation with the ladies…'

He watched the older man struggle with his dignity before capitulating. 'Let's have it, then, son.'

'If you'd like to charm that entire row of women, order them all a pina colada, and then go join them.'

'But I hate those sweet sticky things.'

'You don't have to drink one. You go sauntering up there with something manly in hand, like a Scotch and soda or a brandy. But what will really win their admiration is if you go back to them with gossip…about me.'

His eyes narrowed. 'But I don't have any.'

'You could make it up the way the newspapers do. Or,' he continued when Aubrey started shaking his head, 'I could give you some. And I will. On the condition you make sure Ella takes your seat when she comes back from the restroom. The thing is…' he leaned in closer '… I really need to avoid Adele. She has a gleam in her eye.'

'I thought you'd like that! She's a pretty girl and a woman with a gleam in her eye isn't to be sneezed at.'

Was Adele a set-up? He filed the thought away. 'Normally I would, but I need to clean up my playboy image for business reasons, and Ella has been helping with that—acting as a kind of shield to keep other women at bay.'

'Well, I'll be! You've had us all worried.'

'Of course, Ella and I aren't spreading that around. We want the focus of this coming week to be on Susie and Martin.'

'Naturally.'

'We need to make sure that the bride and groom have a week they'll remember for the rest of their lives. In a *good* way. Ella and I have been putting our heads together to come up with ways to make sure that happens.'

'So *that's* what all this has been about?'

'Absolutely.' People went to hell for lying as well as he did. 'We've been thrown together due to the wedding prep, so we decided to make the most of it. I'm helping endorse her business, and she's helping keep problematic women at bay. Win-win, see?'

'Well, I'll be.'

'Here comes Ella now.'

Aubrey immediately stood, moved into the aisle, and all but manhandled Ella into his seat. 'The poor lad needs protecting from Adele,' he said. 'You look after him, now, you hear?'

She gave a mock salute. 'Aye, aye, Captain.'

Aubrey gestured to a steward and put in his order for five pina coladas and a brandy, and then followed in the steward's wake as they were delivered.

Ella turned towards Harry but didn't meet his eye. 'If you want me to find another seat, I can organise for one of the boys—'

'I asked Aubrey to make sure you sat here.'

She eyed him warily. 'You did?' Then she stiffened. 'Is something wrong? Do we need to go into emergency containment mode or—?'

'It's nothing like that.'

She eased back, pursed her lips. 'So…you'll let me apologise now?'

He nodded, his head suddenly heavy. 'Yes, but—'

'Oh, Harry, I'm so sorry! What I said to you on Sunday was truly offensive. I didn't mean it to be. It came out all wrong. And honestly, it's more of a reflection on me and my insecurities than it is on the kind of man you are. You've shown me nothing but consideration and kindness. And I had absolutely no reason to doubt you.'

'I think you've every reason for those doubts, but we'll get to that in a moment. What do you mean it's a reflection of your insecurities?' The vulnerability in her eyes made his chest hitch. 'What insecurities?'

She stared at her hands. 'I want new friends so badly. I mean, I told you that already. And I'm making them, which feels great.'

He was with her so far.

'I worry, though, that I want it—' Her nose wrinkled. 'This is going to sound so self-absorbed. I worry that I want that more than the people I'm becoming friends with want it.'

His heart lurched. *Oh, Ella, sweetheart.*

'The thought of being too needy and making people uncomfortable... I mean, that'd be awful. When you spoke about clingy women making you feel suffocated.' She shuddered. 'I don't want to be like that.'

'You're not coming across as needy, Ella, I swear.'

She pulled in a breath. 'You've done so much, Harry. You've helped me find my belief in myself again, helped me see that what I'm doing is what I should be doing.' She glanced up. 'You're helping me find my feet with the family again.'

Except that last item was still a work in progress. The conversation he'd just had with Aubrey was proof of that.

'You've gone out of your way to endorse my

brand. I just… I can't see— Please don't take this the wrong way, because I know friendship isn't about what you can get, it's not a financial transaction, but… I can't see what possible benefit my friendship is to you.'

Could she seriously not see her own awesomeness?

'At the moment we're working towards a common goal. We want to make sure this wedding is wonderful. But once we no longer have that point of connection…'

'You thought I'd wash my hands of you.'

She grimaced. 'I had that wrong. I can see now you value friendship every bit as much as I do. What I said on Sunday was me trying to put up a wall so if it did happen and I never saw you again—it would help temper my disappointment.'

He couldn't speak.

'Harry, will you please accept my apology?'

'Utterly and wholeheartedly.'

She sagged. 'Thank you.'

Her words were so heartfelt he suddenly felt small. He didn't deserve them. 'Your honesty slays me.'

'We promised to be upfront with each other. Besides, I was so ashamed of myself when you stormed out on Sunday that nothing less than a full and frank confession would suffice.'

'Do you want to know why I value our friendship, Ella?'

Raising both hands, she shook her head. 'Don't pander to my insecurities. It's not your job to make me feel better about myself.'

'It's because my status, my money, and my accomplishments don't impress you at all.'

'Yes, they do! I—'

'What impresses you is how hard I've worked to achieve what I have. You don't care about the trophies and the trappings.'

Her eyes gentled. 'It sucks that you have to be on your guard around people because you can't trust their motives.'

'Ferociously,' he agreed. 'But you like me for the same reasons I like you—we value the same things, we have the same drive and the same sense of humour, we make each other laugh. And we have the same sense of adventure.'

Her mouth fell open. 'Adventurous, me?'

'What else would you call going out on your own to create Sew Sensational?'

She sat up a little straighter.

Adele chose that moment to amble over. 'Want to swap seats, Ellie? Uncle Derek was hoping to catch up with you.'

'Oh! Harry, we haven't started comparing notes yet on our schedules.'

He grimaced. 'My fault.'

Adele frowned. 'Schedules?'

'We've organised a few activities for the week,' Harry said, pretending to go through his phone.

'I need to tell you about the chat I had with the concierge, Ella.'

'Don't tell me he hasn't been able to organise all the things I asked him to.' She glanced up. 'Give us an hour, Adele.'

Adele drifted away. 'What happens in an hour?' he murmured.

'I fall asleep and you bury yourself in work emails.' She turned more fully to him. 'Speaking of work, did you close the deal with Bright Directions yesterday?'

'I did.'

'Yay! Congratulations. I'm so pleased for you.' She danced in her seat before high-fiving him. 'Lily must be so happy.' She pulled herself back into straight lines. 'Right, so when Adele comes back, hold a finger to your lips to tell her not to wake me and stage-whisper that you've a lot of work to get done.'

'Devious.'

'You're rubbing off on me.'

He settled back in his seat and everything suddenly felt perfect with the world.

CHAPTER NINE

BREATHLESS, ELLA CLAPPED and laughed, as did everyone else on the dance floor. Her father grinned. 'Who knew square dancing could be so much fun, eh, pumpkin?'

It was the end of their first full day in Langkawi, Malaysia, and the first of the planned activities that she and Harry had organised. None of the activities were compulsory. They were simply fun, light-hearted diversions designed to help everyone get into the holiday mood and make the most of their time here. Nobody, however, had sat the square dancing out.

Ella raised an eyebrow and her father laughed again. 'Okay, you and Harrison were inspired. How on earth did you know Aubrey was a square-dance caller?'

'He told Harry when they were sitting together on the plane.' It had seemed a fun way to bring the generations together and create a sense of community among the wedding guests.

'You and Harrison are doing good work here, poppet. I'm proud of you.'

Her old nickname had her eyes filling. 'Thanks, Dad. Susie deserves her dream wedding without the shadow of James's death hanging over it.' She'd never spoken so bluntly before and she held her breath, but her father only nodded.

'You're right. It's time to move on.'

And for the first time in a very long time, it felt possible. They'd always miss James, of course, how could they not? But they could also begin to live their lives again. They could allow themselves to be happy.

'Who are you dancing with next?' he asked, when Aubrey called for everyone to swap partners. 'And where should I set my sights?

The rules were that you couldn't dance with your spouse or fiancé, and you couldn't dance with the same person twice.

'How gallant are you feeling, Dad?'

'*So* gallant. You've never met anyone more gallant.' He pressed a hand to his chest, his eyes twinkling, but then he sobered a fraction. 'I'm totally on board with what you're doing here, Ellie. I'll be as gallant as you need me to be. It's just…'

Her heart beat harder. 'What?'

'It's hard for your auntie Rachel, honey. She wants to give Susie the best wedding, and yet she's afraid we're all going to forget James in the process.'

'That's never going to happen.'

'And she's grieving so hard for all he's missing out on…the life he should've had.'

Her chest clenched. James should've had that life. He'd had the world at his feet. She swallowed the lump wanting to lodge in her throat. 'Which makes it hard on Mum, because it tears her up to see her best friend grieving, and she feels disloyal for wanting to move on…for wanting me to move on.' She pulled in a breath. 'I think Auntie Rachel needs to see a grief counsellor, Dad. And I think Mum should be suggesting it.'

'You could be right. In the meantime, we work on keeping everyone out of the doldrums and having fun.'

Exactly.

'So who do you need me to be gallant to? Who needs some cheering up?'

'Adele.'

His grin widened. 'That girl always needs cheering up. It'll be my pleasure. Oh, and look, here's young Harrison now.'

He clapped a hand to Harry's shoulder, intercepting him from what looked like his next target—Great-Aunt Edith. Wow, that was going above and beyond. Martin was going to owe him big time after this week.

'It must be time for the two of you to actually relax for ten minutes and enjoy yourselves. No doubt you have notes to compare. Keep up the good work.' With a wink, he waved to Adele. 'Look lively, young Adele. I want to see if you youngsters can keep up with a spring chicken like me.'

Harry's mouth hooked up. 'Am I mistaken or did your father just order me to dance with you?'

'Scandalous, isn't it?' she agreed, her pulse picking up pace as they took their place in a square.

'Your dad's right, though. It *is* nice to be able to let the guard down for a bit. Don't get me wrong, I'm having fun, but—'

'All of this vigilance is exhausting,' she agreed.

They hadn't planned to dance together, the memory of the dance at the ball too fresh in their minds, but… 'This is probably good,' she said as they do-si-doed. 'It might've looked odd if we hadn't had at least one dance.' And they'd agreed that they didn't want to do anything that would draw attention to them as a couple.

It shouldn't have been comfortable dancing with him, not when her body came alive at his touch, and heat pooled in places she hadn't known she had as he swung her around and they promenaded. But they had to concentrate so hard on Aubrey's directions, and they laughed so hard when they made a mistake that it… It just felt like letting out a big pent-up breath. 'Extraordinary,' she murmured.

'What is?'

'Just talking to myself,' she said as they led a chain. Before he could question her further, she said, 'Were you about to brave Great-Aunt Edith before my father co-opted you for my dance card?'

'We're a few men short and some of the great-aunts are taking on the men's parts. I thought I'd give them a break.'

He really was a nice man. She squeezed his hand as they went round and round. 'Now I know what Adele and I are doing in the next set.'

His eyes twinkled. 'You're brilliant, you know that?'

Those whisky dark eyes looked at her with so much warmth it made her feel like a million dollars. That was the moment when she really believed that, between them, they could pull this off. They could make sure that Susie and Martin had the wedding of their dreams, and in the process they might even help the family turn their faces towards the future.

They truly were in paradise. Ella moved out onto the deck and down into the shadowed coolness of the garden beyond. A low moon hung in a navy sky, a silver path lighting a sparkling trail to it on an equally navy sea.

'Paradise,' she whispered, welcoming the balmy warmth of the air against her bare arms. She wondered if it ever got cold here.

A few steps brought her to the beach and she

kicked off her sandals to dig her toes into the sand, relishing the sensation, relishing the peace.

Not that it was particularly quiet. The hum of crickets and frogs, the chatter of monkeys and an occasional squawk from a night bird filled the air. But behind it was the supremely peaceful sound of water sighing on sand, and the treetops rustling in the breeze.

A figure emerged from the undergrowth to her left, making her start.

'Everything okay?'

Harry. Pressing a hand to her heart, she nodded.

He moved towards her with that long-limbed ease that made her mouth go dry. She ordered herself to not focus on the moonlight, or the fact this was one of the most romantic locations she'd ever been in. 'All's well. I just stepped out for a moment of quiet.' She gestured towards the recreation room and their party. 'It gets a bit much after a while.'

'You want to be alone? I'll leave you to it and see you back inside—'

'No, no, it's as good a time as any to compare notes.'

They turned to survey their party. One wall of the recreation room was glass, allowing them to see inside, though a proportion of their group had also spilled outside to the deck. Everyone looked as if they were having fun—some dancing, some playing pool. 'I think Susie and Martin are having a good time, don't you?'

'They're having a great time. Your dance lesson was inspired.'

She'd organised for a professional dancer to come tonight and teach them a dance routine to a medley of Susie's favourite songs. 'A few people wanted square dancing again, but it didn't seem fair for Aubrey to miss out on all the fun, and I don't want to wear the poor man out. The dance lesson was the next best thing and right up Susie's alley.' She shrugged. 'It was more of a hit with the girls than the guys, though, so the pool and darts was a nice idea.'

'It's official. We're the best damn bridesmaid and best man on the island.'

They high-fived.

'Right, tomorrow's agenda.' She rubbed her hands together, trying to appear calm and pragmatic...trying to rub away the tingling caused by the palm-on-palm contact. 'We have lots of lazing by the pool or on the beach, plus kayaking for those who want something more energetic. And we need final numbers for the river cruise. So—'

'Before we get to that... How do you think everyone's doing? I mean *really* doing? Susie and Martin are happy, but what about your mother and your auntie Rachel?'

Through the glass wall, she watched her parents move to a table, both holding glasses with little umbrellas in them, to join Uncle Derek, who was nursing a beer. They all looked a little flushed and smiling. 'The break has been really good for my parents.' She cocked her head to one side. 'And Uncle Derek too, I think. I haven't seen any of them looking this relaxed in a long time.' She rubbed a hand across her chest. 'They deserve to have some fun. To be happy.'

'And your auntie Rachel?'

His question speared into all of the sore places in her heart. She searched what she could see of the room and deck. Where was Rachel? She should be there with Ella's parents and Uncle Derek.

Was Rachel in her room in the dark, unhappy and grieving? Ella swallowed. 'She's doing her absolute best to make this a happy time for Susie, but she's not happy. She hadn't been happy since—' A lump stretched her throat into a painful ache. 'Oh, Harry, James wouldn't want this for her, and I don't know what I can do to help.'

Harry turned more fully towards her, his expression grave. 'And how are *you* doing, Ella? You've been putting on a brave face, but it can't be as easy as you're making out.'

Unbidden, tears burned the backs of her eyes. She stared at the room full of happy, smiling people and the world tilted as grief blindsided her. It had been like this in the early days. In those moments when she'd briefly forget James had died, and then remember again. It had always felt like a physical blow. She'd thought she was over the worst of it, but…

'James should be here.' Her voice came out low and vehement, as she gestured at their party. 'He should be in there proud as punch of his little sister and teasing her for her appalling taste in music. He should be in there good-naturedly ribbing Martin and cleaning up at pool. He'd have loved this, and it's so *wrong* that he's not a part of it.'

She gulped back a sob, breathing hard.

Closing her eyes, she counted to five before forcing them open again. 'He should be here but he's not. And that can't be changed. Dwelling on it does no good. And he wouldn't want us to be miserable. If he thought we were moping around it'd horrify him.'

It was the truth and she'd tried to honour that, but… 'He'd want us to be happy. He'd want us to get on with our lives. He'd want us to remember the good times instead of resenting the fact we no longer get a chance to make new memories with him. If we don't move on…' She shrugged, not sure she could explain it. 'It feels as if we'd be breaking faith with him in some weird way and not honouring his memory.'

She pressed her hands to her cheeks, mortified to find them wet. She closed her eyes again. 'I'm sorry, Harry. I haven't…not for a while and…'

He squeezed her shoulder. 'Grief's like that, Ella. You've nothing to apologise for.'

Oh, but she did. *So much.* He had no idea.

'Tell me a good memory.'

She lifted her eyes to the night sky. She'd not allowed herself the luxury of sifting through those, hadn't thought she'd deserved them, but couldn't resist the lure now. A sudden smile shifted through her. 'When I was thirteen, I wanted to make the girls' under-fourteen representative soccer side. James spent three months training with me every afternoon after school. Even though he hated training.'

'Did you make the side?'

'Yep. He made it onto the boy's rep team too, even though he hadn't planned to trial.' She laughed. 'I nominated him without him knowing. He loved to play, but loathed the training. It took him a long time to forgive me for that.'

Harry's chuckle filled the air, and it warmed her in ways that no man—not even James—had done. She reached for another memory. 'Whenever I had a cold he'd make me eat a bowl of chicken soup, and once I'd eaten it he'd then go out and buy me a bag of hot chips, because that's what I craved whenever I was under the weather. He'd then watch my favourite rom coms with me without complaining. It always made me feel cared for.'

She turned to meet his gaze. 'I have a lot of

good memories, Harry.' Could she find a way to remember them without dwelling—?

'Whenever James was feeling under the weather, you'd sneak him chocolate bars and would play endless games of whatever his latest favourite computer game happened to be.'

She swung around. *Auntie Rachel!*

Oh, my God, how long had she been standing there? Had they said anything that might've hurt her? 'I—' She swallowed. 'If anything we just said upset you, I'm really sorry. We—'

'I have a feeling it's me who owes you an apology, Ellie. I've been so resentful towards you for making plans that don't involve James, that I… I've lost sight of some important things.' The older woman stared down at her hands. 'I haven't been fair to you. After all, what else are you expected to do? Stay stuck in some kind of grief rut for the rest of your life?'

She moved forward to brush her thumbs beneath Ella's eyes and dry her tears.

'I'm ashamed to admit it, but a selfish part of me hasn't wanted you to move on. I haven't wanted anyone to move on. But that has to stop. It's not fair to you, it's not fair to your mother. And you're right, it's not fair to James's memory.'

Did she mean that?

'I'd been afraid that you were forgetting James and if you forget him—'

'How could I ever forget him?' She seized Rachel's hands—this woman had been a second mother to her. 'He'd been a part of my life forever. I loved him.'

Rachel pulled her into a fierce hug. 'And a part of me has always known that, Ellie, I promise you. It's just been unbearable to me to consider my life without James in it.'

They eased apart. 'He was your son. Of course it's hard to move on.'

Rachel ran a hand over Ella's hair. 'You said sadness isn't what James would wish for us, and you're right. I don't want to move on without him, but as I heard you talking just now I realised that if I don't I'll be in danger of losing the good memories, and all the good times we shared. If that should ever happen, that's when I truly lose my son.'

'So…' Ella bit her lip. 'You're okay?'

'Yes, my darling girl.' Rachel hugged her again. 'I'm going to be just fine.' She released her and gestured towards the party. 'I'm going to join the group. You?'

A howl started up at the centre of her and she didn't know how long she could keep it in. 'I'm going to take a moment to catch my breath. I actually wouldn't mind an early night.'

'If I don't see you for the rest of the evening, then sleep well.'

Something about the way Ella held herself, the way she pressed her arms tightly to her sides as she watched Rachel return to the party, told Harry all was not well.

The air around her trembled and simmered, and his every muscle tensed. What had he missed? That conversation with Rachel had indicated a turning point. Something Ella had fiercely wished for. She should be happy.

He leaned in close, the scent of peaches filling his nostrils. 'Ella?'

She started as if she'd forgotten he was there, turned with wild eyes. And then she spun away and sprinted down the beach.

What the hell…?

He stared and then set off after her. He understood her need to be alone, but they were in a strange place. What if she got lost or hurt herself?

Her sprint eventually slowed to a jog, and he kept easy pace beside her. Once they reached the end of the beach, she halted and rested her hands on her knees, winded. More from emotion than exercise, he suspected. Eventually she straightened to stalk across and plant herself on a flat rock and stare out to sea.

It was a large rock and he sat down too, uninvited. He knew from experience with Lily that sometimes sitting quietly beside someone could be the comfort they needed. Grief defied logic. He didn't try to press her for an explanation or the reason for her flight.

'I'm such a fraud, Harry.'

His every instinct told him to tread carefully. It was instinct that had saved his neck more than once as he'd negotiated the best route down a mountain, and it was instinct that had won him several world championships. He listened to instinct.

In this instant he metaphorically gripped it around the throat and held on tight, because it felt as if this moment mattered more than any race he'd ever run. Which was an odd notion. He pushed the thought aside. He'd work out what it meant later. 'I think you're one of the most genuine people I've ever met. What makes you say you're a fraud?'

She glanced up and the exhaustion in her eyes made his chest ache.

'Harry, James and I were going to break up.'

He had no hope of keeping the shock from his face. All of this time he'd thought they'd been this mythical golden couple and yet…

'All this time I've been playing the role of bereaved fiancée and it's been a lie.'

He closed his eyes.

'But how can I tell them that? It'd only cause more pain.'

He forced his eyes open. 'He died before the two of you had a chance to tell anyone?'

Her entire frame shook as she drew in a breath. 'James died before the two of us could have that conversation.'

'Hold on.' He shook his head to try and clear it. 'You and James hadn't discussed it yet?'

'I know how it sounds, but I knew James almost as well as I knew myself. When I told him I wanted to leave the firm to set up Sew Sensational…'

'You disagreed.' He remembered her mentioning that. 'But, Ella, some people are risk-averse and it takes them longer to—'

'It made us both realise that we wanted different things in life, Harry.' She met his gaze once more, her smile heartbreakingly sad. 'And I realised I couldn't sacrifice my dream so he could have peace of mind and security.'

She stared back out to sea. 'And I know he was wrestling with all of that too. He'd always dreamed of running the family firm with his wife and passing it on to his children—a real *family* business.' She stared down at her hands. 'He always swam more when something was troubling him. He said it helped to quieten his mind—like meditation—and that in the quietness he could get to the heart of a matter. Find a way forward.'

Skiing could be like that too. His heart burned, though, that this was Ella's final memory of a man who'd obviously loved her as much as she had him.

'If he hadn't been so troubled about us, he wouldn't have been out swimming at such an early hour.'

'He was a fool to be swimming when it was still dark and there wasn't anyone else around.'

She stiffened. 'Lots of people do it.'

'Doesn't make it right. He should've taken more care.'

She spun on the rock. 'It was an accident. He didn't mean for it to happen!'

'Exactly.'

He saw the moment she registered his meaning. She turned back to stare at the sea, her lips pressed into a tight line.

'Ella, James's death wasn't your fault either. You need to stop blaming yourself.'

She still didn't turn.

'And I'll tell you another thing. You hadn't had the *"Are we staying together or breaking up?"* conversation with James yet, so, while you might've known him as well as another person can know someone else, you can only hypothesise on how the conversation would've gone. You can't know for sure.'

She turned back. 'I—'

'What if those early morning swimming sessions were him finding a way to work your new dream into your lives? What if he was reimagining your futures so you could both have what made you happy?'

'You can't know—'

'Neither can you!'

She blinked.

'Oh, Ella, do you really think the man who, as a thirteen-year-old, trained with you for three solid months so you could reach the dream you had then, was really going to ask you to give up your adult dreams? Do you truly think he wouldn't have done all he could to make sure you could follow your Sew Sensational dream?'

She swallowed.

'No doubt you took him by surprise and threw him for a loop, but do you truly think he was ready to throw in the towel?'

Her face crumpled and with an oath he pulled her into his arms as sobs wracked her body. 'Oh, sweetheart.' She'd been bottling these awful thoughts up and her guilt had been eating her alive.

He held her close, stroked her hair, and murmured meaningless nothings in the hope they'd soothe her. He'd do anything to take away her pain. Eventually the tears subsided, but she didn't move—she remained in his arms as if she didn't have the energy to move.

And God help him, but he loved the feel of her there, her warm weight pressing against him, the scent of peaches rising up all around him.

'Thank you,' she whispered.

She eased away and he immediately missed her warmth. It took an effort not to pull her back against him. 'You don't need to thank me. I—'

'You've given James back to me.'

He stilled.

'And you've no idea what that means. Everything you just said is so true. I've been playing worst-case scenarios, tormenting myself. The thought that I'd somehow blighted his last days has haunted me. I...' She shook her head. 'Just like Auntie Rachel, I'd lost perspective.'

She met his gaze. 'I don't know if James and I would've made it as a couple or not, but you reminded me of one crucial fact. James was my best friend, and I was his. We wanted the best for each other. And that's one thing we never lost.'

He traced a finger down her cheek, and her breath hitched. 'He wouldn't have wanted you haunted in any kind of way.'

'No,' she agreed, her gaze dropping to his mouth and hunger stretching through her eyes.

Her face filled his vision, and roaring sounded in his ears. It was as if a strange force gripped him, one he had no control over. Their gazes met and held, he lowered his mouth towards hers— need, desire and craving flooding his every atom. Their breaths mingled, the air sawing in and out of their lungs, only a few centimetres separating them...

He froze. What the hell was he doing?

Look where you are. You're on a public beach. Anyone from their group could walk by!

He shot to his feet.

She blinked and then stood too, one hand

pressed to her ribs, just beneath her breasts as if she were trying to catch her breath. She glanced from him and then quickly out to sea. 'I'm sorry, Harry. Talk about sending you mixed messages.'

There'd been nothing mixed in what he'd read in her eyes. She'd wanted him with a fierceness that thrilled him. 'No apologies necessary. It's been an emotional evening.'

She turned, hands on hips, chin set at a defiant angle. 'The things that have happened tonight, Harry...they've freed me. I no longer feel guilty for wanting you. And I do want you. I'm tired of pretending I don't. I want to spend the night with you.'

He tried to wrestle the temptation back under control, tried to stop it from dragging him under. 'Two things,' he ground out.

She folded her arms. 'Okay.'

'We're not spending tonight together.'

Her face fell.

'If you were to regret it in the morning, I'd feel like a heel. You're vulnerable right now. I can't take advantage of that.'

She opened her mouth as if to argue, but then her shoulders slumped. 'While I think you're wrong. I don't want to make love with you if you're worried about that. It wouldn't be fair.'

Damn, he liked this woman.

'And the second thing?' she asked.

'The wedding.'

She turned away, raked both hands through those glorious curls.

'I know your auntie Rachel turned a corner this evening, but if word was to get out that you and I had…'

'It would cause…consternation.'

'And we don't want to do anything—'

'To ruin the wedding,' she finished, turning back to him.

He took a step towards her. Her eyes widened and the pulse in her throat fluttered like a wild thing. It took all of his strength not to press a kiss there. 'But come Monday, everyone leaves and we're here for another week. If you still feel the same way then…'

'I'll still feel the same way,' she said with a flattering swiftness that had him needing to anchor his feet more firmly on the sand.

He bent so they were eye to eye. 'Then you and I are going to spend some serious one-on-one time together in my cabin come Monday and I'm going to make you come so hard and so often you're going to cry Uncle.'

She leaned in closer until their breaths mingled. 'Challenge accepted. And we'll see who's actually crying Uncle by the end of the week.'

He went so hard he saw stars, and then he laughed. 'In the meantime I'm going to need a lot of cold showers.'

They walked back to the resort and had barely

set foot on the deck when Ella's mother came racing up. 'My darling girl, Rachel told us about the conversation the two of you had. She's turned a corner and I'm so grateful.'

She folded Ella in a hug. Her eyes narrowed when she pulled away and stared into her daughter's face. 'You've been crying!'

'I'm fine, Mum. It's just been an emotional night, and poor Harry here copped the brunt of it. I'm sure I soaked his shirt.' She shrugged. 'I hadn't known I'd needed to turn another corner too, that's all. But I feel better now.'

Harry found himself enfolded in a hug then too. 'Thank you for being there for my daughter, Harry.'

She'd called him Harry not Harrison. He swallowed an unexpected lump. 'It was nothing. Ella is special. I'm proud to call her my friend.'

'And we're sorry, sweetheart,' her father said, moving to stand with them. 'From now on you get our unconditional support for Sew Sensational. We want to support you in anything that makes you happy.'

Ella's eyes filled. 'Thanks, guys, that means a lot.'

They shared a three-way hug and he could feel a grin—no doubt ridiculously goofy—break across his face.

'We're heading to bed,' Mr Hawthorne said. 'We'll see you in the morning.'

They watched the older couple stroll through the garden in the direction of their cabin, arm in arm, and Ella swung round to him. 'Just…wow. I'd have never achieved all of this on my own, Harry. Thank you. Thank you to the power of a million!'

She hugged him then and it made him feel like Superman.

CHAPTER TEN

EVEN THOUGH ELLA was minutely aware of Harry during her every waking moment, and, if her tangled sheets every morning were anything to go by, her every sleeping moment too, the next couple of days passed in a blur of fun and laughter and sightseeing.

Not that she and Harry saw those sights. For both the kayaking on the lagoon and the boat tour to explore the inland river system that they'd organised, more people turned up for the events than who'd registered interest, meaning they had to give up their slots.

'Don't even think about it,' she told her parents when they realised what had happened.

'But you organised it and your mother and I know you were looking forward to it.'

'There'll be time for sightseeing next week,' she told them.

The older couple exchanged glances. 'We were going to save this for when the wedding was over, poppet, but I think now is as good a time as ever.

We've paid for you to have a beachside cabin next week. We thought the extra room would come in handy for your filming. It's our way of apologising and to let you know we truly do support you.'

'Oh, but—' Ella stared from one to the other. 'That's too generous. It's—'

'Nonsense!' Her mother hugged her, and so did her father.

Ella had to blink hard when they eased away.

'Now don't let her go back to her room and sew, Harry,' her mother ordered. 'She deserves a holiday too.'

'I'm going to stretch out on that gorgeous beach with a magazine, and I plan to spend at least an hour bobbing about in the sea. I might even have a snorkel,' she told them.

'Sounds fabulous,' Harry said. 'Count me in. A lazy few hours is exactly what the doctor ordered.'

'The two of you have been working so hard behind the scenes. Don't think it's gone unnoticed. Ask the kitchen staff to pack you a picnic.'

Harry grinned and it made her heart beat too fast for comfort. 'This is sounding better and better.'

They waved everyone off and headed back to the resort. 'Where are you going?' Harry demanded when she turned in the direction of her room.

'I thought that with everyone out of the way, I might...'

He folded his arms and raised an eyebrow.

Okay... 'Harry, after last night and how...um... *tense* things got, I thought maybe you wouldn't want to spend too much one-on-one time with me.'

He straightened. 'Are you worried I won't be able to control myself?'

She sent him a self-deprecating grin. 'Unfortunately, I know you can.'

He spluttered out a laugh and then sobered. 'While we plan to become lovers, don't forget we're friends too. I enjoy spending time with you, Ella. I don't feel as if I'm treading water or biding my time. The plan you just outlined to your parents sounded like a fine one to me.'

Oh. She couldn't find her voice at all.

'You need to learn to live in the moment, learn to make the most of your downtime. Becoming a workaholic won't help Sew Sensational in the long run.'

He had a point.

He nodded in the direction of her quarters. 'So where are you going?'

She swallowed. 'To grab my towel, a hat, my magazine and the sunscreen.'

'Perfect. I'll meet you back here in five.'

She couldn't believe how easy the next few hours were. She and Harry read, swam, chatted, swam some more, and ate a delicious hamper the resort's kitchen staff had whipped up, and for the first time in weeks, maybe months, she felt herself truly relaxing.

'I had no idea Malaysia was so beautiful.'

Palm trees lined a white sand beach, and they reclined in the shade of one now. Behind them was the lush greenness of the tropical rainforest where long-tailed macaques—small mischievous monkeys—waited for opportune moments to try and raid their picnic hamper.

Their conversation moved to the beautiful places they'd visited, and she listened spellbound as he described his favourite alpine locations. He made them sound like magic. Maybe when Sew Sensational was making a tidy profit she could visit them for herself.

After lunch they snorkelled the shallow bay, marvelling at the brightly coloured fish, and for the life of her she couldn't remember a more perfect day.

As soon as everyone returned from their excursions they were 'on' again. Cocktails by the pool and dinner were followed by an evening of trivia. There was a *Susie and Martin* category and a lot of joke prizes that kept everyone laughing.

Friday had been deemed a rest day—in preparation for the wedding the following day—so more lazing by the pool ensued, but she and Harry had concocted plans for a water fight. As prearranged, he threw the first water bomb, hitting Ella squarely in the chest as she reclined on a banana lounge. Martin's shot went a little wide of Susie, but when it burst it splattered both Susie and her cousins, making them all shriek.

Ella handed out oversized water guns and the older folk strategically retreated to an upper level of the veranda. From their positions above, Edith and Aubrey acted as generals, shouting out instructions to the group as the girls waged war on the guys. Of course, everyone ended up in the pool playing a rowdy game of volleyball.

From the other side of the net, Harry winked at her. She grinned back.

Friday night, however, was their *pièce de résistance*—karaoke. Family night karaoke. There wasn't a whole lot of rhyme or reason to it. Everyone and anyone could join in with whatever song they wanted. Uncle Derek sang The Temptations' 'My Girl' to Susie, making everyone sniffle. Susie and Martin started up *Grease*'s 'Summer Nights' and nearly everyone joined in—the women behind Susie, skipping and dancing, while the men lined up behind Martin, strutting and acting cool.

Ella fanned herself afterwards. Harry could really move when he…um…wanted to.

When the mums led everyone in 'Dancing Queen', though, Harry and Ella, who'd retreated to the back of the room for a breather and to sip their sodas, high-fived each other. It was a moment of perfection, everything she'd hoped for and more. When Auntie Rachel gestured for her to join them, she pushed her drink into Harry's hand and ran up onto the makeshift stage to dance with them, aware of Harry's gaze on her the entire time, warm with desire.

She danced for him, and couldn't wait until Monday came and they were finally alone.

'How do I look?'

Susie turned from the mirror to face Ella and the mums. All three of them drew in audible breaths. The mums' eyes filled. Ella blinked hard. 'You look like perfection, Susie. Utter perfection. You're going to knock Martin's socks off.'

She fussed, adjusting a strap, smoothing the skirt at the back. The dress was simple—shoestring straps, a ruched bodice of white silk encrusted with crystals. The skirt fell in soft folds to Susie's feet and the sheer chiffon overlay drifted around her when she walked. With her hair piled on top of her head and falling around her face in ringlets, she looked beautiful.

Oh, James, I wish you could see her.

'Thank you, Ellie. For everything.' Susie grabbed her in a fierce hug. 'This week has been everything I dreamed it would be.'

Ella hugged her back. 'There's nothing to thank me for.' She eased back and winked. 'And I hope this coming week exceeds all your dreams too.' After this evening's celebrations, Susie and her groom were being whisked off to their own private honeymoon hideaway on the other side of the island for a week.

Susie grinned, her cheeks going a delicious shade of pink.

The ceremony was beautiful, and as the happy couple exchanged vows Ella shared a glance with Harry. He smiled, those whisky eyes warm with approval. She could practically read his thoughts when he nodded towards Susie and Martin—*We did it*. She sent him a surreptitious thumbs-up from where her hands were wrapped around her bouquet. Then they both turned to the front with huge grins and watched their dearest friends exchange rings.

Saturday afternoon and evening were a time of joy and celebration.

Sunday was a day of rest and relaxation. And packing. Everyone except Ella and Harry was leaving the following day. Though Ella packed up her room too in preparation for moving to the beachside cabin. The cabin had separate living and sleeping quarters, which would make it perfect for setting up the two sewing machines the resort had sourced for her.

By mid-morning Monday, she and Harry were finally alone. As they waved everyone off, she felt unaccountably shy. He turned to her with a grin. 'I've organised a surprise.'

He had? Before she could grill him, he said, 'You'll need your swimmers, a hat and decent walking shoes.' And just like that, her nerves vanished.

Half an hour later she found herself standing at the bow of a privately chartered boat, sailing along the Kilim River, staring in awe at the towering treetops that passed either side of them. Her guidebook had told her that the area was rich with mangrove swamps, lagoons, pristine beaches, and rock formations, but to experience it first-hand was magical. Wildlife was abundant too and their guide pointed out swimming macaque monkeys, hairy-nosed otters, and sea eagles.

When they emerged into a bay and a vertical limestone formation rose up in front of them—ancient, majestic and breathtaking—all she could do was stare. Its sheer cliffs towered above everything, dominating the landscape. 'Thank you for this, Harry,' she whispered. She'd remember it forever.

'You deserved a treat. For the last week you've been looking after everyone else—organising tours and activities, spa treatments and banana lounges, cocktails and canapés. You've made sure that everyone has had the most wonderful time.'

'You worked just as hard.'

'I knew how much you wanted to explore the river. It didn't seem fair you should miss out.'

She had to swallow before she could speak. 'You didn't need to—'

He pressed a finger to her lips. 'Humour me.

For the next few days I don't want you to worry about a thing. It's time you let someone spoil you.' He leaned closer. 'And I believe I'm the perfect person for the job.'

Harry watched the expressions dance across Ella's face—surprise, awe, delight—and was fiercely glad he'd organised the river tour. The hungry, ravening part of him had wanted to drag her off to his lair and make love with her all day, again and again, until they were both too drunk on pleasure to move.

But Ella deserved more. She deserved to be wooed. And while he recognised the answering hunger in her, she didn't deserve to be rushed. He'd sworn to take his time.

They were going to become lovers, but they were friends too and that friendship was important. They'd take their week here, they'd make love and he'd be her transitional man, help her move on to the next stage of her life, and when they returned to Sydney and normality, they'd still be friends. He wanted her to know that, to feel it in her bones and trust in it. He wanted Ella in his life for good. She'd become the best damn friend he'd ever had.

They ate their lunch on a deserted beach, sitting on a blanket on the sand in the shade of the forest. Ella's eyes widened when she saw the label on the bottle of champagne. 'Harry! That's a little extravagant.'

'Not today. Nothing's too good for today.' He poured two glasses and handed her one, raised his own. 'To us.'

She touched her glass to his, her lids fluttering in appreciation when she took a sip. 'Oh, my. It's delicious.'

He stared at the wet sheen the champagne left on her lips and heat rose inside him hard and fast. He anchored one hand in the sand and gestured towards the picnic hamper with the other. He *would* go slow. 'More deliciousness awaits.'

She lifted the lid. 'Right, so… We have some gorgeous sourdough bread, prawns and shellfish…salad.' She stilled. 'Mangoes and little strawberry tarts.' Her gaze lifted to his. 'All my favourite things. How did you know? Who did you grill?'

He stretched out his legs, tried to stop her expression from sneaking under his guard and doing weird things to his heart. 'I didn't have to grill anyone. I've simply paid attention.'

Her eyes grew suspiciously bright. She blinked fiercely, stared back down at the food he'd ordered. 'You should've added a creamy Havarti, crackers and olives, and salt and vinegar chips.'

She'd been paying attention too?

'Thank you.' Those bright blue eyes held him

momentarily captive. 'It's been a long time since anyone went to this much trouble for me.'

He would *not* ravish her. Swallowing an oath, he reminded himself that she deserved finesse, and Egyptian cotton sheets, and a king-sized bed. She deserved a man who would go slow.

He *could* go slow.

He *would* go slow.

He eased away from her a fraction. 'I want you to be able to look back on this week with...'

'With?'

'Affection. I want the memory of it to always bring a smile to your face.'

'And will you? Will you look back on this week with affection as well?'

Her words made his mouth dry, though he didn't know why. 'Every time I hear the word Malaysia, it's going to make me smile, Ella. That I can promise you.'

It was a day of diamonds and gold.

As Harry dressed for dinner that evening, though, he found it harder and harder to bridle the passion that rampaged through him. He'd hopefully given Ella a day she'd remember forever. He couldn't spoil it now. He *would* be patient while they shared a candlelit dinner, he *would* be controlled while they danced to something sweet and smoky. Only then would he bring her back to his cabin and lavish her with the single-minded attention she deserved.

He pulled in a long breath, fixing his purpose in his mind.

He turned at the tap on his door—open to take in the glorious view outside. Ella stood in the doorway. 'Can I come in?'

'Of course.' He gestured her in, trying to banish the image of the king-sized bed in the neighbouring room from his mind.

She wore a silk shift dress in bright turquoise and when she walked it moved over her body like water, highlighting the curves beneath. He bit back a groan. 'You look lovely.' He swung away before he lost his mind, dragged her into his arms and kissed her senseless. 'Drink?'

He marched over to the bar fridge. Would it be inappropriate to go take a cold shower? Was there even water cold enough in the world to dampen the heat rising through him?

When she didn't answer, he glanced back, and instantly straightened. The way she bit her lip and twisted her hands… What was wrong? How could he help?

He froze. Had she changed her mind? Acid burned his stomach. If she had, he'd act like an adult.

The frown in her eyes deepened. 'Do you mind if I say something?'

'Not at all.' His voice emerged too low and gravelly, but he couldn't help it. If she'd changed her mind he'd behave like a gentleman. He clenched his jaw. She deserved nothing less.

'It's just that we've fallen into the habit of being honest with each other and...' She shrugged. 'I like that. I like that we don't play games with one another.'

His shoulders unhitched a fraction. If nothing else, he had this woman's friendship. He valued that friendship, trusted in it in a way he rarely trusted anything. He wouldn't allow sex, or the lack of it, to come between them.

'It means a lot to me too,' he assured her, moving to take her hands. 'So tell me what's on your mind.'

He had a feeling that she wanted to remove her hands from his. His fingers instinctively tightened. *Finesse. No pressure.* He loosened his grip and then didn't know what to do. He couldn't bring himself to release her completely. He settled on continuing to hold her hands lightly instead. If she wanted to break the contact, she could. He wouldn't stop her.

'Harry...'

He loved the way she said his name.

'If you're having second thoughts...'

What?

She winced and he realised he was crushing her fingers. He immediately relaxed his grip.

'I just wanted to say that if you are, then I understand and you don't need to worry about hurting my feelings. We're both adults and—'

'*No.*'

She eyed him uncertainly. 'No, we're not adults? Or no, you're not having second thoughts?'

She pulled her hands from his and pressed them to her abdomen. It pulled the silk at the front of her dress taut, highlighting the rise and fall of her breasts. He couldn't wait until he could run his fingers down their sides again to elicit those breathy, needy gasps. He let his gaze linger and heat, and her nipples beaded in instant response.

Only then did he lift his gaze back to hers. 'I'm not having second thoughts, Ella. Are you?'

She shook her head, pink flushing her cheeks, but the frown in her eyes remained. 'Then why the withdrawal?'

'I haven't withdrawn! I'm simply trying to keep a rein on my baser instincts. I want to make this week special for you. I don't want you to feel rushed or *stampeded.*'

'Oh, for pity's sake,' she murmured under her breath, before pulling herself up to her full height. Which still wasn't all that tall, but it didn't stop her from looking as regal as a queen. 'I know you've had a lot more experience at this kind of thing than I have, but we're still equal partners, right?'

'Of course.'

'I have as much a say as you in what happens here?'

'Absolutely.' How could she think otherwise?

'Good,' she said, before turning and walking to the door.

Hold on! Where was she—?

She closed the door and he swallowed as she leaned back against it, an unconsciously sensual temptress.

'The thing is, Harry, I don't want to wait any longer.'

She pushed away from the door and reached under her arm to draw down the long side zip of her dress, and the sound of it lowering filled the sudden hush of the room. His breathing sounded loud in his ears. She shimmied the dress over her hips and it fell to pool at her feet in a splash of colour.

His groin hardened in instant approval, his nostrils flaring as he greedily surveyed her lingerie.

She moved towards him. 'Do you approve?'

Approve what? No longer waiting? Of the lingerie? Either way, his answer was the same. 'Wholeheartedly. You look…' There weren't any words to do her justice. 'Beautiful.'

Beneath her turquoise jewel of a dress she wore a lace bra and panties in a vivid tangerine, and the sight made his mouth dry. She'd been fake tanned to within an inch of her life—her words—earlier in the week, and she glowed with a golden good health that had his every atom firing to life. He stood rooted to the spot as she hip-swayed towards him with the grace of a tropical nymph.

Halting in front of him, she slipped a finger beneath one bra strap. 'I made these with you in mind.'

She'd *made* them?

'The colour is called Tropical Heat. It's how you make me feel, Harry—like I'm on holiday one minute and then as if I'm going to burn up the next.'

He couldn't resist her then. He caught her mouth in a raw greedy kiss that spoke of his need, and she kissed him back with a hunger that set him on fire.

Deep drugging kisses.

Hands dragging at clothes.

She pulled back, breathing hard. 'Do you mind if I…?' She gestured at his shirt.

He shook his head. She could do whatever she damn well pleased.

Gripping his shirt in those small strong hands, she pulled and the buttons popped and flew all around them. She gave a delighted laugh. 'I've always wanted to do that.'

How many other button-down shirts had he brought with him? He made a mental note to buy at least another twenty from the resort gift shop tomorrow.

'I'll sew them all back on tomorrow.'

Not a chance. He meant to keep her far too busy for anything as mundane as sewing on buttons.

All thought fled then when her hands ran across his chest, revelling in the feel of him. Before he could lose all the strength in his legs, he swept her up in his arms and strode into the bedroom. Laying her down, he immediately covered her body with his.

'Trousers,' she gasped. 'You need to lose the trousers.'

He didn't answer. Instead he took one nipple into his mouth and laved it with his tongue as he ran the backs of his fingers down the sides of her breasts and back up again. She gasped and arched into him, his name dragging from her throat.

He moved his way down her body, learning all the things that made her gasp and moan and arch into his touch. Only then did he shuck the rest of his clothes and seize a condom. She went to take it from him as if to sheath him herself, but he shook his head. 'I'm hanging on by a thread here, sweetheart.'

'Please tell me that means you're not going to make me wait any longer?' she said, her voice threaded with need.

He settled himself back over her. 'No second thoughts?'

'None whatsoever.'

He entered her in one smooth stroke and her mouth opened on a long sigh, her body arching up to meet his. Their gazes caught and clung. 'That was definitely worth waiting for,' she whispered.

He huffed out a laugh. *She* was worth waiting for. All thought fled then as she moved with him in a rhythm that seemed all their own. Her muscles gripped him, tightening as the heat and need built, until she cried out and they were flung out into the abyss, finding release together.

CHAPTER ELEVEN

ELLA DIDN'T KNOW how long she lay there afterwards, her fingers entwined with Harry's, a kaleidoscope of colours dancing behind her eyelids as she waited for the world to resume its normal course on its axis.

On the pillow beside her, she felt Harry turn his head to look at her. She opened her eyes and turned to meet his gaze.

'That was—' he said.

At the same time she said, 'Wow!'

Chuckling, he pulled her to him and she curled against his side, her head on his shoulder and her hand making patterns across his naked chest, her fingers revelling in the firm, vibrant feel of him.

He pressed a kiss to her hair. 'Are you okay?'

'Absolutely!' Why wouldn't she be? She felt alive in a way she never had before. She lifted her head. 'Are you?' Was there some post-coital etiquette she was unaware of because she and James had never had any other lovers and, hence, had made the rules up as they'd gone along?

He grinned and she let out a breath because he certainly looked okay—all sated smugness… happy and relaxed.

He twirled one of her curls around his fingers, brought it to his lips. 'I love these.'

That made her smile.

'I'm *very* okay. I'm about as okay as it's possible to get.'

The way he looked at her did crazy things to her breathing.

'But I also know I'm the first man you've made love with since James, which makes this a milestone of sorts. And milestones shouldn't pass unacknowledged.'

The man looked like a Greek god, he made love with an intensity that could become addictive, but it was his kindness that really caught at her. 'Oh, Harry.' She pressed a kiss to his chest. 'It's past time I moved on—we both know that. These last couple of days, all of the attention I've had left that the wedding hadn't taken from me has been focussed on you. There's not been any other thought in my head.'

His eyes darkened at her words. She reached up and smoothed a hand across his cheek. 'I know how much effort you've put into making this experience wonderful for me—and you've achieved that. I'm never going to forget this for as long as I live. Whenever I do think of it—' she had a feeling she'd be pulling this memory out a lot '—it's *always* going to give me a happy shiver.'

She pretended to frown.

'What?' he demanded, his muscles bunching beneath her fingertips.

'And hot,' she added. 'Very, *very* hot.'

He instantly relaxed, that grin hooking up one side of his mouth and sending her stomach tumbling. His grin disappeared, though, when her fingers danced down his abdomen, her hand drifting lower and lower.

'Ella.'

She didn't know if it was a warning or a plea. 'You're an excellent lover, Harry. You swept me away completely, had me mindless with pleasure as you explored every inch of my body. I didn't get the opportunity to explore every inch of you.'

His groin twitched back to admirable life. She stared at it, her mouth going dry. She forced her gaze back to his. 'And I'd very much like to.'

He blinked as if she'd surprised him. His expression gentled as he reached out a finger to trace her cheek. 'I want to make you happy, Ella. I want you to have whatever you want this week. But you don't have to—'

She closed her fingers around him and his words ground to a halt and a guttural groan ground from his throat. She grinned, and a lascivious heat licked along her veins. 'Then how about you lie back and think of England while I...explore?'

His breath hitched as she pressed a path of kisses across his chest and down his stomach, across firm muscle and hot male flesh. His hands clenched in the sheets. 'Ella!'

She paid him no heed. Her mouth closed over him and his hips jerked. She took her time before lifting her head. 'Whatever I want, you said. Do you want me to stop?'

His eyes had turned smoky and slumberous. She recognised the desire darkening his eyes and pulsing in her hand. 'No, but I want to make this good for you and—'

He broke off with a low groan as she resumed her ministrations. 'You can let me take care of that, this time.'

She took the lead, taking her time exploring him with the same slow focus that he had her, and when she finally sheathed him and straddled him, she was as hungry and needy as him. His hips surged upwards as if he were unable to control his need and her muscles clenched around him. They found a rhythm that all too soon had her crying in release and wonder, his cry following immediately after.

He caught her when she collapsed to his chest in sated exhaustion. Holding her to him, he rolled them to their sides with a surprised oath that sounded like an endearment.

* * *

The following day they were boated out to spend the day on a tiny uninhabited island—just the two of them in an idyllic tropical wonderland. They returned in the evening to a candlelight dinner on the beach. The day after, he took her to a local village where they spent the morning with batik artisans. She returned with so much batik fabric she'd need to buy another suitcase to get it all home.

And they made love. She hadn't realised before the many different moods lovemaking could take—playful and spontaneous, raw and needy, intense…and loving. The first time they'd met, Harry had told her they were on the same wavelength; that never felt more true than when they were making love.

He looked after her in every way imaginable. It was as if he wanted to fill her with every good thing—infuse her with joy and strength and wonder—so that when she returned to the real world she'd have the resources to move forward with her life with confidence.

In odd moments she'd wonder how, once they returned to Sydney, they'd return to being just friends—wouldn't they continue to burn for each other with the same fire they did now? But she'd push the thoughts away. Harry had done this before, and he didn't seem to have any qualms.

No doubt work and the ordinary world would consume them once again, and they'd find their friends' footing once more. And even if that didn't happen seamlessly, they were adults, and their friendship meant a lot to them. They'd work at it.

Harry hadn't become a world champion by giving up. And she wasn't the kind of person who surrendered the things that mattered either. Sew Sensational proved that. They'd find a way to make it work.

'Lil said she'd be here at six p.m.'

Lily had texted Harry from the airport and he'd organised dinner for the three of them at eight o'clock, but he'd wanted to greet her when she arrived. His closeness to his sister touched Ella. She'd tried to absent herself, had thought it'd be nice for him and Lily to have some sibling time, but he wouldn't hear of it.

'Lily's expecting to see you too. She's so excited about the filming.' He sent her a smile that made her blood fizz. 'Thank you for indulging her.'

'I'm as excited as she is.'

From inside the foyer, they watched as the resort minibus pulled into the circular driveway. 'This should be her now.'

He started for the foyer door, but pulled up short when Viggo emerged from the minibus behind Lily. Ella's gut clenched at the expression on Harry's face. He didn't like Viggo? 'Smile,' she ordered. She'd ask questions later.

His eyes swirled with turmoil. 'Did you know about this?'

'No, but, regardless, you don't want to disappoint her.'

His nose curled. 'I suppose you're right.'

'And you don't want to make Viggo feel uncomfortable.'

'I don't give a damn about Viggo,' he ground out, just as the new arrivals marched into Reception. The moment Lily clapped eyes on Harry she flew into his arms.

And then she hugged Ella too. 'Isn't it wonderful? I talked Viggo into joining us.'

'This is a surprise,' Harry said, offering his hand to the other man.

'But a good one, right?' Lily said, hanging off Viggo's arm and practically dancing where she stood.

Ella surreptitiously kicked Harry's ankle. He straightened. 'Absolutely.'

But some of the excitement drained from Lily's face as if she sensed Harry's mood. Ella jumped in. 'We've arranged to have dinner on the beach at eight o'clock. I hope that suits. It gives you nearly two hours to freshen up and get into holiday mode.'

Lily started to dance again. 'Sounds wonderful.'

'We'll let the kitchen know to set a fourth place. So, we'll see you soon.'

'Can't wait,' Lily said as Ella practically dragged Harry away.

'What is wrong with you?' she said when they'd

reached his cabin, planting her hands on her hips. 'You know the two of them have been dating. And I know you're protective of her, but she is a grown-up.'

He paced to the door and scowled out at the beach. 'I don't trust that guy.'

She moved to wrap her arms around his waist, nuzzled his neck, and he rumbled his appreciation. 'Why not?' she asked. 'He seems like a nice guy—a little reserved, perhaps, but from the little I've seen he treats Lily like a queen.'

He turned to wrap his arms around her, drawing her closer, and her body came to instant eager life. 'You think I'm being an overbearing big brother.'

'I think you're being a tad overprotective. You need to loosen up, though, or you're going to put her back up.'

He let out a breath that caught at her. 'I don't want to see her get hurt.'

'Of course you don't. But you don't get to tell her who she can and can't date. Besides—' she pressed herself more fully against him '—she's entitled to a bit of fun, a bit of R & R, just like we are.'

That made him grin. 'What time did you say dinner was—eight p.m.?'

She nodded.

'That gives us over an hour. What could we do in an hour?'

She cocked her head to one side and pursed her lips. 'Hmm... I wonder.'

He laughed low in his throat and kicked the door shut. 'Let's find out, shall we?'

They made it to their table on the beach at three minutes past eight, Ella slightly breathless, to find Lily and Viggo already seated. 'Isn't the resort and the island gorgeous?' Ella said, sliding into her chair.

Lily's gaze shifted from Ella to Harry and back again, and her eyes started to dance. In that moment Ella knew any hope she and Harry had of trying to keep what was happening between them a secret had just flown out of the proverbial window.

'It is the epitome of a tropical hideaway,' Viggo said in his heavily accented English.

'Magical,' Lily agreed. Her smile turned mischievous. 'The air here certainly seems to have agreed with the two of you.'

Ella's cheeks heated and she hoped the gathering darkness hid her blush. 'It certainly has. It's been far too long since I had a holiday and my mind is buzzing with ideas for our filming. Though that will only take an hour here and there. You'll have plenty of time to explore the island and get some R & R.'

Lily leaned forward, her lips curving in excitement. 'Viggo and I have managed to extend our holiday. We're now staying a full week.'

Her original plan had been to stay for only three nights.

Harry blinked. 'I thought you were swamped with work.'

'I was, but I made time because…'

'Because?'

Something hard had entered his voice. Ella glanced at Lily's shining face, and then at Harry's frown and an awful portent gathered beneath her breastbone.

'We have the most exciting news, Harrison. Please be happy for us. Viggo has asked me to marry him. And I've said yes.' She gave a happy squeal. 'We're engaged to be married!'

Wow. Before Ella could offer her congratulations, Harry leaned forward and stabbed a finger to the middle of the table. 'Are you out of your minds?'

He shot to his feet and the smile dropped from Lily's lips. Viggo rose too, calm and stern, moving to stand behind Lily, his hands on her shoulders in a show of comfort and solidarity. The expression on his face informed anyone who cared to look closely enough that he wouldn't allow anyone to upset his intended, not even her overprotective big brother. 'We hoped you'd be happy for us, Harrison.'

Ella tried to tug Harry back into his seat, but he was as immovable as a snow-covered mountain. No, not snow. The heat rolling off him was the antithesis of winter. At the moment Harry was more a seething volcano.

'Harry,' she whispered, hoping to break through whatever red mist had descended over him.

He ignored her. 'Have the two of you thought about this? *Really* thought about it? It means— You know what it means and—'

'Yes,' Lily and Viggo said in unison.

'But—' He broke off, glanced at Ella, frustration twisting his features. With an oath, he turned and wheeled away, disappearing into the thick foliage of the garden.

Ella stared after him, her mouth dropping. Snapping it closed, she swung back to the happy couple. 'I'm really sorry about Harry,' she said as Viggo resumed his seat. Not that it was her place to apologise for him. 'But a huge congratulations to you both. I think it's the loveliest news.' She filled their glasses with the champagne sitting on ice and proposed a toast. 'To the two of you—may you have a long and blissfully happy life together.'

Lily's eyes misted with tears. 'Thank you.'

They drank.

'You're not going after him,' Lily whispered.

'Absolutely not!'

'But the two of you seem…close.'

She pondered that. 'This might sound crazy, but in the short time I've known Harry, he's become—' she shrugged '—the best friend I didn't know I needed.'

She hoped Lily got the message. She and Harry might've become lovers, but they were friends first and foremost.

'So?'

She pushed her shoulders back. 'So he just behaved badly.' *Why had he behaved so badly?* 'And I've no intention of pandering to it.'

She pasted on her best smile. 'Besides, I'm hungry and the seafood here is amazing. I suggest we have a lovely dinner to celebrate your gorgeous news. And I want to hear all about Viggo's proposal. Was it romantic? Tell me all.'

Lily's face lit up. 'Oh, Ella, you've no idea. It was *so-o-o* dreamy.'

Harry paced the living room of his cabin, glaring at the clock. Ten p.m.! Where the hell was Ella? He'd checked her cabin twenty minutes ago, but she hadn't been there.

He seized his phone from the nearby counter to check it for the umpteenth time. No text messages. He slammed it back down. *Damn.* He thought they were friends! Apparently, though—

A knock on his door had him swinging around. Ella stood framed by the light in a deceptively simple dress with some kind of sheer overlay that floated on the breeze. Every cell in his body responded, roaring to life with hunger. He did what he could to ignore it. 'Where the hell have you been?'

It came out more savagely than intended. Not that she flinched. Not that she gave off much of anything. He couldn't stop pacing.

'I take it that means I can come in?'

'You don't need an invitation, Ella. Not after everything we've been getting up to these last few days. We'd agreed you could treat this place as your own.'

She moved inside, sat on the sofa with teeth-gnashing calm. 'You asked where I've been. I've been doing what you should've been doing. I was having dinner with your sister and celebrating her lovely news.' She stood again. 'But rather than gritting your teeth and pretending you were happy for her, you flew off the handle like an idiot—'

An idiot!

'—who bitterly disappointed her.'

He swallowed.

'And hurt her feelings.'

His stomach churned.

'And marred something that was precious and special.' She strode across and poked him in the chest. 'You were rude, ungenerous…' she hesitated '…and unkind.'

The bottom dropped out of his stomach.

She moved to the refrigerator and grabbed them both cold sodas. 'You might not approve of her chosen man, but you don't get a say in who she marries.'

'But—'

'No buts. If you don't want to materially hurt your relationship with Lily, you'll find her first thing tomorrow and apologise. And try to find some reasonable explanation for why you behaved so badly.'

She'd taken a seat on the sofa again and he fell into the one opposite. 'You really thought I was unkind?'

'Uh-huh.'

He could tell she was disappointed in him and that stung, mattered more than it ought to. 'Look, Ella, there are things you don't know.'

'Like the fact Viggo is minor royalty of a small Scandinavian kingdom?'

They'd told her? *Wow*. 'Minor? Damn it, Ella, he's third in line to the throne.'

'But once both of his older brothers have babies, he'll drop further down the line of succession pretty quickly.'

She leaned forward, elbows on her knees. Her neckline fluttered in a delicious vee that hinted at the shadow of her breasts. He forced his gaze upwards.

'Lily thinks you were angered by her news, but I know better. That wasn't anger. It was fear. What I don't understand is what you're afraid of.'

His jaw dropped. What the hell…?

She gestured between them. 'It's the wavelength thing.' Her frown deepened. 'So what gives?'

All of the anger seeped out of him, leaving him spent. 'If Lily marries a man like Viggo, she's going to be thrust into the spotlight. We know what the papers are like. They don't judge women by their accomplishments or what they achieve, but by what they wear and how well they present themselves. For most of her teenage years, Lily battled demons surrounding her weight and what she looked like. This is the last environment I would wish for her.'

'Oh, Harry.' Every sign of reserve drained from Ella's face and she flew across to sit beside him, her eyes warm with sympathy and her hand warm on his arm. 'I should've realised. You're worried that being thrust into the spotlight will trigger all of her old insecurities.'

He tried to smile, but he couldn't, not when his insides were twisted with so much *fear*. If he were to lose Lily... He closed his eyes. He didn't think he could bear it.

'Harry, you're forgetting something important.'

He forced his eyes open.

'Lily is an adult now.'

'Do you really think that makes a difference? Ella, when my parents divorced, it nearly destroyed her. She idolised my father, and I thought he idolised her too—loved her. Hell, I thought he loved me, and I was pretty damn gutted when he cast us off like last year's fashions. But I was older, had started to work out the kind of man he was.' And he hadn't liked what he'd discovered.

He dragged a ragged hand down his face. 'We were supposed to be her haven, Ella. She'd been through so much. We were supposed to be something she could believe in again. But we let her down.'

Ella's eyes filled with tears. 'Harry, you didn't

let her down. You've never let her down.' She placed her hand over his heart. 'I know you're worried that Viggo might break her heart the way your father did. And that if he does it'll send her spiralling into despair and depression.'

Exactly!

'But do you think wrapping her up in cotton wool and hiding her away from the world is the answer?'

'Of course not.' He rolled his shoulders to stop her words from settling there. 'It's just…if anything goes wrong it'll be ten times worse if it happens when she's in the public gaze.'

'And what if it never happens?'

He leapt up to pace again, agitation making his gut churn. 'There are too many variables and—'

'And there are some constants you're not taking into account.' From her spot on the sofa, she held her hand out to him. 'Come and sit again.'

He hesitated, but did as she bid.

'Lily is an adult now and that does make a difference. She's learned strategies to cope with those old insecurities. She knows now that she's not to blame for the breakdown of your parents' relationship. She's not that same scared and confused teenager. And the fact she wants to head up your initiative with Bright Directions proves that.'

Her words made sense, but—

'There's always a risk when falling in love, but it doesn't mean the risk isn't worth taking. And,

Harry...' She paused until he met her gaze. 'She loves Viggo. Truly loves him.'

That fear speared into his gut again.

'But Viggo loves her too. Fiercely, I believe. This is a risk for him as well. And he's not a rash man.' She hesitated. 'You're mistaken if you think he's ignorant of her past. I'd bet you a million dollars that they've discussed it.'

Did she think so?

'One more thing and then I'll shut up. Whatever your thoughts, feelings and opinions are on the subject, you're not going to change her mind about this. Or Viggo's.'

He felt the truth of those words in his very bones.

'So if you don't want to alienate her...'

'I need to apologise.'

'Grovel is the word that immediately leaps to mind.'

He winced.

She leaned in until their eyes met. 'More importantly, you need to tell her why you behaved the way you did, and what it is you're worried about.'

He groaned, dropping his head to his hands. 'God, I made a real hash of it tonight, didn't I?' He lifted his head. 'But I can do a really good grovel.'

'Good to know.' But there was a smile in her eyes too.

She was right. If he wanted Lily to forgive him, she needed to know why he'd acted like such a brute. Seizing his phone, he sent Lily a text. An answer pinged back almost immediately. 'She's agreed to meet me for a walk before breakfast.'

'Excellent.'

'And, apparently, if that goes well, I can join her and Viggo afterwards.'

'Where you can finally toast the happy couple.'

He pressed his lips together tightly and nodded. Tomorrow he would think before he spoke.

'You were right!'

Harry burst into Ella's cabin the next morning. She glanced up from her laptop and her eyes lit up—at the sight of him or his news, he had no idea. 'Everything went well, then?'

He picked her up and swung her around. 'Very well. All three of us spoke very frankly and—'

He broke off to drag a peach-scented breath into his lungs.

She thumped his arm. 'And?'

'They're setting strategies in place in case it does start to feel too overwhelming for her. Viggo has a palace full of staff at his beck and call, including counsellors of the highest calibre. The palace is happy to let him and Ella take a back seat in terms of royal duties now that his older brother has married and the first grandchild is on the way. Viggo and Lil plan to focus on their charity work and to divide their time between Scandinavia and Australia.'

'Sounds perfect.'

'I was an idiot to fly off the handle the way I did.'

'You were an understandably concerned big brother,' she said staunchly.

Her loyalty touched him.' He twined one of her delectable curls around his finger. 'You told Lil I was your best friend.'

She blinked as if surprised she'd come up in conversation. 'I know we've only known each other for a short time, but…well, that's what it feels like. Harry, you bolstered my confidence in Sew Sensational at a time when I was considering surrendering that whole dream. You helped me help make Susie's wedding dream come true. You helped me encourage the family to turn their faces towards the future. And…'

She dragged in a breath that made her entire frame shudder. 'You've helped me move on too—helped me stop feeling guilty about James, helped me to embrace my own—' her cheeks went pink '—needs. I'm free and happy, and that's all down to you. I'm lucky you came into my life when you did. So, yes, Harry, you're my best friend. I don't know what else you'd call it.'

Sincerity shone from her eyes and he couldn't utter a single damn world, an odd lump blocking his throat. So he did what he ached to do. He leaned down and kissed her.

CHAPTER TWELVE

THE NEXT COUPLE of days were a revelation. Ella hadn't realised the creative rush one could get when three other intelligent people were invested in ensuring her videos were the best they could be. What she thought would only take an hour, often blew out to encompass an entire morning or afternoon due to everyone's enthusiasm.

They filmed a series of fifteen-minute workshops on how to repurpose old sarongs to make a beach caftan, a sweet little shirt, and a beach bag. Lily sewed alongside her to demonstrate the simplicity of the makeovers, but to also highlight where the inexperienced sewist could become unstuck. Harry and Viggo discussed how to get the best lighting and what were the best camera angles.

It was a ridiculous amount of fun.

Everything had worked out so *perfectly*. She'd been so disappointed at missing the expo, but the promotional work Harry had done for her—wearing the waistcoats, introducing her to the kind of people who set trends, not to mention guesting on her channel—had more than made up for it. The filming she was doing now with Lily, coupled with the networking she'd embarked upon herself, would consolidate all of that hard work.

Her name was getting out there, Susie had had the wedding of her dreams, and now Ella could attend the expo next year *with* her family's blessing. A month ago she couldn't have envisaged such a happy outcome.

When they weren't working on her videos, the couples went their separate ways—exploring the island or lazing on the beach—coming together for dinner each night.

And the nights themselves were... She swallowed, a familiar heat rising through her. The nights were a revelation.

Making love with Harry was utterly exhilarating. Maybe it was the short-term nature of their liaison that had her embracing it with a zeal reserved for once-in-a-lifetime events. Whatever the reason, it felt as if the stars had aligned. She felt as if she was on the path she'd always been meant to travel.

And if thoughts intruded for how they would go back to being *just friends* when they returned to Sydney, she pushed them out again. They had no place in the week, and she refused to let them mar what little time they had left.

'Ella, I've had a thought.'

She glanced up as Lily skipped into the cabin.

'What if we were to film a kind of preview here in Malaysia that you could release once Viggo and I announce our engagement officially? Viggo doesn't want to appear on camera, but I could talk about the engagement, my mother's wedding dress and how you're going to help me alter it to make it mine? It'd be fun, don't you think?'

Ella's jaw dropped. 'You still want me to work on your dress?'

'Of course.' Lily frowned. 'Why wouldn't I?'

Harry sat up from where he loafed on the sofa. 'Maybe because you're going to be a princess, Lil, and the palace will no doubt want a say in everything to do with the wedding.'

'They can content themselves with dressing Viggo, choosing the church and the guest list. *I* get to choose my own dress and who I want working on it.'

This would catapult the Sew Sensational brand into the stratosphere. 'Lily?' She leaned towards her. 'You're sure about this?'

'Positive.' Lily hugged her. 'You've given me a vision for the perfect dress—*my* perfect dress— and I'll feel as if I have my mother there with me on the day, and that means so much to me.'

Viggo had walked in behind Lily and stood leaning against the walls in the shadows. 'She wants to film this right away, so when the palace sees it—and when the people see it—they will want her to wear this dress too. She wants to create a human element that will have them all falling in love with her.'

Lily lifted her chin. 'I just want people to see I'm an ordinary girl who's excited about her wedding and marrying the man of her dreams.'

Ella recognised the flicker of concern in Harry's eyes as they rested on Lily and wanted to ease it. She also wanted to bring Lily's vision to life—not just the dress, but how she wanted Viggo's fellow countrymen to see her. Lily wanted to take control of her destiny and Ella would do everything she could to support that.

She thought hard, her business training coming to the fore. 'Okay, let's not overthink this. How about we start with a basic conversational format? I'll start us off by asking you some questions and we'll see how we do. We'll keep going even if we stumble—we can edit those bits out later—and we'll see what we come up with.' She glanced at Viggo. 'We can edit out anything the two of you decide you'd rather not have go to air. I'm happy for the palace to vet it too if need be.'

Viggo waved that away. 'I trust you, Ella. I know you won't sell this to the tabloids.'

'We all trust you.' Harry grinned at her with so much warmth it made her feel the centre of the world.

She dragged her gaze away to survey Lily. 'You're camera ready.'

'I came prepared, hoping you'd say we could do this now. You, however, need a lick of mascara, a little powder on your nose…and go put on that gorgeous wrap dress.'

With a laugh, she did as Lily bid.

Half an hour later, they were well into the interview. It had been so ridiculously easy. Lily was so happy she shone, and Ella tried to stay as much in the background as she could as Lily spoke of her engagement and Viggo's romantic proposal.

Slowly, though, the tables started to turn when Lily confided to the camera that the first time she'd met Ella, she'd fan-girled all over her. 'I'm so grateful we met, and it was just by chance because of my brother.'

Ella smiled into the camera. 'Some of you will remember Harry from the feature I did on waist-coats. We were best man and bridesmaid at our dear friends' wedding, which is the whole reason we're in Malaysia now.'

'Harrison is one of the kindest people I know,' Lily said. 'He's been one of the biggest influences in my life. I honestly don't know where I'd be without him.'

From the corner of her eye, she saw Harry straighten. *Way to go, Lily.* Between the two of them, they could further rehabilitate Harry's reputation in a piece of video that had the potential to go viral. 'I couldn't agree more. He has a heart of gold.'

Lily pulled in a breath. 'He helped me through one of the most difficult times in my life.' And Lily then spoke of her struggle with the eating disorder she'd developed at the age of twelve, and how Harry's strength and patience, and his unwavering belief in her, helped her to win that battle.

It was the perfect lead into a discussion about Harry's partnership with Bright Directions, but first... Ella moistened her lips. 'He helped me through a really difficult time too, reinforced my belief in myself and my dream of opening a sewing school at a time I was on the brink of surrendering that dream. I owe him so much. He's become one of my dearest friends.'

She was about to steer the conversation around to Harry and Lily's joint charity work when Lily said, 'I think he's more than a friend, Ella. I think you're in love with him.'

The shock of those words doused her in ice, held her immobile for several long seconds. Seconds that felt like years. She wasn't in love with Harry. She couldn't be. *No!*

Then she recalled that the camera was rolling and forced a laugh. 'I will confess that I might have a teensy crush.' She pressed her hands to her heart. 'Those shoulders!'

They both laughed and Ella steered the conversation to the wedding dress and twenty minutes later they finished up.

She glanced across at Harry. He'd moved to stare out of the window, and even from here she could see the tension that had his spine rigid and shoulders stiff. She winced.

Damn!

Damn. Damn. Damn.

'Ooh, can we look now?' Lily said, bouncing over to Ella's laptop. 'We could—'

'We have other plans for the rest of the day,' Viggo said, taking her hand, evidently aware of the undercurrents in the room. 'We're going snorkelling off the reef.'

'But—'

'I'll send the raw file to you right now to watch whenever you want. You can suggest edits and we'll take it from there,' Ella managed. 'Have a nice time out on the reef.'

The silence that descended when Lily and Viggo had left had her breaking out in gooseflesh. She rubbed her arms, trying to lift the numbness that had her in its grip. She swallowed. 'Harry?'

If possible, he went even more rigid. *Oh, God!* He was feeling suffocated, wasn't he? They'd been having so much fun and because of her stupidity he now couldn't breathe. And due to his innate kindness—that soft heart he did his best to hide—he now felt guilty and responsible and just like his father.

He swung around. 'Is it true?'

If there'd been a single doubt in her mind that

he might feel the same way, it died a swift death now. She rubbed a hand across her chest, but it did nothing to ease the ache that gripped her.

'We promised each other honesty, Ella.' Those whisky eyes flashed. 'Have you fallen in love with me?'

'Yes.'

He flinched, his face draining of colour.

'I didn't realise until the moment Lily said it. I suppose I'd have worked it out once we were back in Sydney, but...' She trailed off. There didn't seem to be much more to say.

'You promised!' he burst out. 'You told me just because you'd fallen in love with one friend didn't mean you'd fall in love with another.'

'I didn't mean for it to happen! I didn't *know* I was falling in love with you.'

He paced the room, flinging his arms out. 'How can you not know you're falling in love with someone?'

'I don't know,' she shot back, stung. 'Why don't you try it some time and then maybe you'll be able to explain it to me.'

Her words made him freeze.

'Of course, that's never going to happen because the moment you start to feel something real for someone, you head for the hills.'

His head reared back as if she'd slapped him.

'I will, however, tell you one thing, Harry.' She folded her arms tight across her chest to stop from

reaching for him. 'I have absolutely no expectations of you.'

His gaze speared to hers.

'I'm asking nothing of you, so you've absolutely
no reason for all of this outrage. I might've fallen
in love with you but I'm not *clingy*. I've zero expectations of you falling in love with me.' Her
heart clenched. 'And from the expression on your
face I'm not holding out great hopes for our future
friendship either.'

His head rocked back again.

She dragged in a breath. She wouldn't cry. Not
yet. 'This thing between us ends right now.' If he
couldn't promise her friendship, she didn't want
any of the rest either. *Liar*.

'Darn tootin', it does.' But his voice lacked its
earlier heat.

She thrust out her chin. 'And if you think I'm
going to curl into a little ball and hide my weepy
self from the rest of the world you're going to be
sadly disappointed. I've a lot to look forward to,
and a lot to keep me busy. This is just a…*bump*.
I already know broken hearts mend.'

Oh, she was going to cry buckets and buckets
over this man, but he didn't need to know that.

'And just for the record,' she added, 'I don't
regret a single second of—' she gestured around
'—any of this.'

She wanted to tell him that if he had the cour-
age to unlock that heart of his for more than five

minutes, he might discover that for himself. But what was the point? He wouldn't believe her.

'I know you think you're a carbon copy of your father, Harry, but you're not. It's just a lie you tell yourself to keep your heart safe.'

His jaw dropped.

She reached across to grab her beach bag and towel. 'If you'll excuse me, I'm going to go lie on that gorgeous beach and make the most of what's left of this holiday while I can.'

She turned and left, not lifting a hand to brush away the tears that had started to fall down her cheeks, in case he watched. She had no intention of letting a single gesture betray how shattered and broken she felt. He already felt bad enough. She didn't want to add to his guilt and regret.

Harry stared after Ella as she walked away and tried to make his mind work.

Damn!

He swore hard and loud and with a vehemence that shocked him. How had he not seen what was happening? How could he have *let* it happen?

His hands clenched and unclenched. He needed to go for a run and clear his head. Actually he needed to ski at breakneck speed down a mountain, but there weren't any convenient Alps in the vicinity. And even if there were, it was August.

You could book a flight for Switzerland this afternoon. There'd be a dribble of snow somewhere.

It was what he'd normally do—head for the hills as quickly as he could.

But if he did that he'd ruin—

Ruin what? There's nothing here left to ruin. The thought made him want to drop his head to his hands and yell out his frustration as loud as he could.

Go for a run.

He turned to leave then stopped and glanced around. Ella had walked out without packing up any of her computer equipment. Anyone could walk in and take it. He shifted his weight from one leg to the other, before moving across to her computer. He emailed the raw video files to Lily and Viggo…and himself, before shutting her computer down and placing it in the safe in her bedroom, along with her purse and phone, neither of which she'd taken to the beach with her.

Only then did he let himself out of her cabin to go pull on a pair of running shoes.

He ran hard and long. He might no longer be in the peak physical condition of a world champion, but he could still run hard and fast. For a long time. Even in heat and humidity.

But he couldn't outrun his thoughts.

So he dived into the sea and tried to outswim them, but that didn't work either. Eventually he stumbled up shore to collapse against the trunk of a coconut palm and wait to dry off, wait for his heart rate to slow.

Why hadn't he taken more care where Ella was concerned? She wasn't built like him. He'd always known that. For pity's sake, she'd had one other lover—the man she'd meant to marry! He'd always made it a rule to never get involved with a woman like that. Why the hell had he made an exception this time around?

Because he'd thought they were on the same wavelength.

His nostrils flared. Because he'd *wanted* to believe they were on the same wavelength.

He dragged both hands through his hair. He'd been so damn selfish. He'd let desire override everything else. In exactly the same way as his father.

The realisation had him battling nausea. For more than half his life he'd worked hard to be the opposite of his father. When he'd discovered that the same restlessness resided in his veins, the same antipathy to commitment, he'd made sure to not become involved with anyone who would read anything more into sex than a temporary release.

And he'd succeeded.

Until Ella.

And Ella was the last person who should have to deal with heartbreak. She'd had enough to deal with for the last year and a half, and she had big plans. She needed all her energy to see those plans through. If he'd done anything to derail them...

He leapt up and started to pace.

Seizing his shirt and sneakers, he trudged back in the direction of his cabin. Was there some way he could fix this? Could he mitigate the damage somehow?

A growl sounded in the back of his throat. He'd do anything!

He showered. He lay on his bed and stared at the ceiling fan going around and around. Endlessly. Going nowhere. And wondered if he'd ever felt more wretched.

Smothering a curse, he seized his laptop and downloaded the video file, watched Ella in action. It hurt just to look at her.

The thought of losing her friendship had a ball of pressure building beneath his breastbone that threatened to break him in half. He clenched his hands and forced himself to keep breathing, forced himself to watch that moment when Lily had claimed Ella was in love with him.

The stricken expression in Ella's eyes, so brief, when she realised the truth stretched his throat into a painful ache. 'I'm sorry, sweetheart.' He brushed a finger across her face on the screen. 'I'd have not hurt you for the world.'

At some point he fell into an uneasy sleep. He woke with a start to pounding on his door. The shadows in the room had lengthened, and he sat up, groggy in the semi-dark, his eyes feeling scratchy and his skin hot and tight.

'I know you're in there, Harrison!'

Lily. He fell back against the pillows to stare at the ceiling again. He made no move to get up and open the door. He didn't want to talk to Lily. The only person he wanted to talk to was Ella.

Lily gave up and left.

The only person he wanted to *see* was Ella.

He froze. In the past, whenever a woman told him she'd started to develop feelings for him, the claustrophobia would descend, smothering him in a suffocating blanket that sucked all the joy and light from his world. He'd have to throw it off as quickly and efficiently as he could or risk losing his sense of self.

But that sense of suffocation hadn't descended over him this afternoon.

His phone pinged. A text from Lily: You're an idiot!!!

'Tell me something I don't know,' he muttered.

Setting the phone down, he tried to work out why he hadn't felt smothered and trapped by what had transpired this afternoon. He switched on the bedside lamp, but it didn't help shed any light on the dark places inside him.

Ella hadn't begged him to give them a chance. She hadn't tried to change his mind about love and commitment. She hadn't tried to curtail a single one of the freedoms he considered essential to his happiness.

She hadn't apologised for falling in love with him, but she had told him she hadn't meant to.

She'd said she didn't regret a single thing that had happened between them. And she'd told him he was nothing like his father.

His hands clenched. If he weren't like his father, none of this would have happened in the first place!

I wouldn't have hurt your mother for the world.
Hadn't he thought the same thing about Ella?
Then fix it. Don't hurt her.

The thought made him flinch. As if that didn't have disaster written all over it. He hauled himself off the king-sized bed and headed for the shower again. Cold water might help clear his head. He couldn't risk doing to Ella what his father had done to his family. Ella wanted children and if—

The image of a curly-haired little girl lodged in his mind, making him ache.

You're not like your father.

She believed that. They'd never lied to each other. He lifted his face to the cold jets of water. She was wrong, obviously—

He stilled, his mind suddenly whirling.

But what if she wasn't?

He turned off the jets, stood there dripping.

He hadn't thought of another woman since he'd met Ella. It was odd, but true. Despite his supposedly infamous wandering eye, the only woman he'd noticed in the last six weeks had been her.

He'd expected to have to work hard to toe the celibacy line—and obviously he hadn't managed it. But where previously he'd have been captured by one bright smile here and the flash of a different pretty thigh there, that hadn't been the case. He hadn't been tempted by countless lovely women...just one.

He seized a towel, blotted his face. He'd only wanted Ella's attention. He *still* wanted Ella's attention. Even after she'd told him she loved him.

He rubbed the towel over his hair. Did he really think he'd eventually get bored with her? Ella was the kind of woman a man could know for a lifetime and she'd still manage to surprise him. She'd still be able to make him laugh in twenty, thirty, fifty years.

And feel cared for.

He halted. Ella had always made him feel cared for. And that feeling... It was the best feeling in the world. Even better than flying down a mountain at breakneck speed. Did he really mean to cut himself off from it?

It hit him then. He hadn't felt suffocated when she'd said she loved him. He'd felt cast adrift when she'd walked away.

CHAPTER THIRTEEN

LILY'S PHONE PINGED with an incoming message and Ella tried to not look too relieved at the brief respite as Lily checked it. She, Lily and Viggo were all trying to maintain a bright flow of conversation over dinner, but all Ella wanted to do was crawl back to her room and hide under the covers. When she'd tried to bow out of dinner, though, Lily had been so crestfallen she'd found herself backtracking.

Ella hadn't mentioned Harry once, but clearly she hadn't needed to. Lily had taken one look at her face earlier in the afternoon and had read it all. 'I'm so sorry,' she'd said. 'I shouldn't have said anything. I just wanted to shake Harry up.'

Well, she'd certainly done that.

'I just want him to be as happy as Viggo and I are. And, Ella, he *is* happy with you.'

Not in *that* way, though, and the knowledge sliced at her with the cold precision of a rotary blade. 'What we had was always temporary, Lily. I knew that.' She'd gone into their arrangement with eyes wide open. 'Besides, people find happiness in different ways. You need to let Harry find his own happiness.'

Lily's eyebrows rose now as she read her message, and then she sent a quick message back before setting her phone face-down on the table. 'I'm sorry. I always promised myself I wouldn't be *that* person—the one glued to their phone at the dinner table. I promise not to look at it again.'

Ella forced a smile to uncooperative lips. 'What do the two of you have planned for tomorrow?'

Viggo and Lily exchanged a brief glance. 'We haven't decided yet.'

Oh, no, no, no. She wasn't letting them look after her. She might have a broken heart, but that made her neither feeble nor helpless. 'After hearing how much the two of you enjoyed exploring the reef, I thought I'd head out on the snorkel boat tomorrow.' It was one of the many activities the resort offered. 'Weren't you thinking of chartering a yacht?'

A waiter placed their entrées in front of them. The food smelled delicious, and the presentation couldn't be faulted, but her stomach gave a sick roll. She doubted she'd be able to force down a single bite.

She set her napkin on the table. 'I'm really sorry, guys, but I have a splitting headache. A touch too much sun, I suspect. I think I need to lie down in a dark room and let it pass.'

Before she could rise, however, Harry strode into the restaurant…in a dinner jacket, no less. The sight held her immobile. *How unfair!* How was she supposed to maintain a modicum of equilibrium—and pride—when the man looked like *that*?

He spotted them and started directly for their table. Ella glanced at Lily. 'The text you just received. It was from Harry?'

Lily picked up her phone and showed her the conversation.

I AM an idiot.

Told you so.

Are you in the restaurant? Is Ella with you?

Yes, and yes.

Harry *wanted* to see her? Now that was something she hadn't expected. She pressed her hands together in her lap to stop them from shaking. It didn't mean anything. This could just be his attempt to save their friendship.

But as she watched him stride closer, she suspected her feelings were far too strong for her to settle for friendship. She had a feeling she couldn't settle for anything less than Harry's heart. But giving his heart to any woman was a concept that was totally foreign to him.

He halted at the table, but he didn't sit. 'Hello, Ella.'

'Harry.'

Viggo took Lily's arm and rose. 'I believe this is our cue to leave.'

'Oh, but—' Lily spluttered.

'Thank you,' Harry said, over Lily's protests. 'I appreciate that.' His gaze met Ella's again. 'May I take a seat?'

The gentleness of the question had tears burning the backs of her eyes, and she realised that Lily and Viggo were waiting for her to answer before they made their exit, so she nodded. 'Of course.'

As soon as Harry said what he needed to say, and she'd heard it like the adult she was—she gritted her teeth and repeated the word *adult* over and over in her mind—she'd plead a headache and retire for the night. She *could* manage that much.

He leaned across the table towards her. It had seemed like a perfectly respectable-sized table when she, Lily and Viggo had been sharing it, but it shrank now. 'I owe you an apology.'

She glanced out of the window with its glorious view of the beach—palm trees silhouetted against a full moon, no less—and her hands clenched. 'Do we have to do this, Harry?'

'Yes.'

Fine. Then… 'You don't owe me an apology. What happened this afternoon shocked us both. Neither of us meant for it to happen. You're not responsible.' He might never see it, but he wasn't his father. 'I harbour no anger towards you.'

Please let him be satisfied with that.

'I harbour anger towards myself.'

She stiffened. She was tired, cranky and, whether he'd meant to or not, he'd broken her heart. 'You want *me* to make *you* feel better? Seriously? I'll amend what I just said—I *do* harbour certain…hostile feelings.'

His brows rose. 'Hostile feelings?'

Was he laughing at her? She shot to her feet, clenching her hands so hard she shook. She knew she was drawing glances but she didn't care. 'I'm not hungry so I suggest we take this outside where I can yell at you properly.'

He immediately rose. 'Whatever you want.'

Ha! That was a joke. What she wanted wasn't on the table.

Without another word, she whirled on her heel and marched to the nearest exit. Which, of course, led down to that ridiculously romantic beach with its silver sand and those rotten palm trees, big moon and all of that starlight. It made her want to scream.

Kicking off her sandals when they reached the sand, she left them where they fell to march down to the waterline, needing to stay in motion.

'Tell me about these hostile feelings of yours.'

She rounded on him. 'Are you laughing at me?'

'No, I swear. But let me have it, Elle. Don't hold back.'

She wanted to tell him not to call her that, but she loved the sound of the diminutive on his lips. The way he said it sounded like an endearment... and then she saw her sandals—silly strappy things—dangling from his fingers, and all the fight went out of her.

He'd picked up after her?

He noticed her staring at them and shrugged. 'They're pretty. I figured you wouldn't want to lose them.'

She'd never be able to wear them again. They'd always remind her too strongly of this moment.

'Tell me why you're angry with me. I think you should be angry at my general cluelessness, for not seeing what was happening.'

She turned away. Then she'd have to be angry with herself too.

'And for the infantile way I reacted this afternoon.'

She turned back, planting her hands on her hips. 'You know what really offends me? The fact that you think I'm going to fall apart because I have a broken heart. You think I'm going to go off the rails like poor Lily did when she was twelve. But guess what, Harry? I'm not a child and I'm not without resources.'

She hiked up her chin. 'I'm strong.' She swallowed. It might not be easy, but... 'I will get over you. In the meantime I'm going to make a roaring success of Sew Sensational, I'll spend time with new friends, and eventually I'll even start dating again and—'

'*No!*'

'My life will be full and happy and every good—' She broke off, her eyes narrowing. 'What do you mean...*no*?'

'I mean I don't want you dating anyone else. I only want you to date me.'

Her heart thudded so hard she feared it'd leave bruises. Had he just said...?

'I love you, Ella.'

She took a step back. Didn't he know lying to her was a hundred times worse than anything else? 'Don't you do this. Don't you dare.'

'Do what?'

To his credit he did look suitably confused.

'You have such a horror of being like your father, you'd be prepared to shackle yourself to a woman you didn't love to ease your conscience and prove—'

'I'm nothing like my father!'

She rocked back on her heels. Fire flashed from his eyes and he mangled the straps of her pretty sandals in his fist. She suspected he was rendering them unwearable, but she couldn't care less about her shoes. She cared about the fire in his eyes.

'All of my adult life I've done everything I could to not be like my father, without realising the very impulse rendered me the antithesis of who he is.'

Wow. Okay. That was progress. 'I'm glad you can see that.'

'And you know what else? I finally realised that my animosity wasn't due to the fact that he divorced my mother and broke up our family. Divorce happens, people change, and I wouldn't wish a loveless marriage on anyone. But he constantly betrayed her, was unfaithful to her—not just once, but many times. Infidelity is...' He shook his head. 'It's a terrible thing to do to a person who trusts you.'

She agreed wholeheartedly.

'Worst of all, though, was the way he abandoned Lily and me. Shed us like an old suit he had no use for any more. He made no attempt to fit us into his new life.'

Her shoes dropped to the sand as he took several steps away. Her heart burned at the slump of his shoulders, at the way he raked both hands back through his hair.

'He didn't *want* to fit us into his life. He didn't love anyone but himself.'

She rested a hand against his shoulder, aching to offer him some comfort. 'I'm sorry, Harry.' The man should be hung from his thumbs.

He turned. They stood too close. She should

take a step back, but the expression in his eyes held her immobile, his heat and scent twining around her, casting a spell in the moonlight.

He thrust out his jaw. 'But *I'm* not like that. I love Lily. I love my mother. I love a lot of people—the team I trained with for years and friends like Martin.' His eyes danced. 'In a manly, masculine kind of way, of course.'

'Of course,' she said, her lips twitching and her heart lightening at the expression in his eyes.

'And I love you, Ella. Not just as a friend. I love you with all of my heart.'

Her breath hitched and she took an involuntary step back, but his eyes didn't waver from hers.

'I know I panicked earlier.'

He could say that again. She folded her arms, but she didn't know if it was to protect herself against his words or her own violent reaction to them.

'But it wasn't because I felt suffocated. And it wasn't because I couldn't breathe.'

She found that she was the one who now couldn't breathe.

'It was because I thought I'd hurt you and the thought sent me mad. I couldn't think of any greater crime I could possibly commit.'

She wanted to weep. She didn't want his guilt and remorse. And that was all this was, and—

'I wasn't thinking of me. I was thinking only of you.'

Which was the antithesis of his father. She understood that. But it didn't mean he loved her.

'And when you walked away, Ella—and don't get me wrong, I don't blame you for walking away—it wasn't relief that flooded me, relief that you'd given me an out and had let me off the hook…all without creating a scene. I felt…'

He paused until she met his gaze once more.

'I felt lost.'

Her heart all but stopped.

'It took me a while to work out what it meant. You said you hadn't realised you'd fallen in love with me, so you can't hold my own cluelessness against me. I've always thought my restlessness and lack of interest in settling down meant I wasn't designed for the long haul, but I was wrong. It just meant I hadn't met the right woman yet.'

Did she dare believe him?

He leaned in close. 'You're my best friend but you also send so much heat flooding through my veins that there are times I can't think straight. But I'm thinking straight now.' He touched a finger to his temple and then hers. 'The same wavelength, that's us. You and I have never played games and I'm not playing games now. I want it all with you, Elle—the friendship, the sex, but most of all the love. Every single day of our lives together is going to be an adventure—the best adventure I could ever have imagined.'

She couldn't breathe, couldn't move.

'So what do you say?' He gave her one of those devilish grins. 'Do you dare take a risk on a guy like me? Because make no mistake about it, Ella. I'm talking forever here. And I know there are still a few hurdles in our way. We'll have to take things slow for your family's sake—let them get used to the idea of you having a new man in your life. And the press won't believe that I've settled down and will try to cause mischief.'

He'd thought about this. Really thought about it.

'But we just need to wait those things out. And, together, we can do it. I know we can.'

He pulled in a long steady breath. 'Here's the thing. I'm through with being a coward with my heart.' He straightened and spread out his arms. 'It's all yours if you still want it.'

She didn't hesitate. She stepped into those arms and stood on tiptoe to stare into his eyes. 'I love you, Harry. I will always love you. And I promise to keep your heart safe.'

He grinned—one of those huge numbers that did that crazy thing to her pulse. 'There's not a doubt in my mind. You?'

'None,' she breathed, pulling his head down so she could kiss him with all the love in her heart before she burst from it.

He kissed her back with a wonder and joy that had tears pricking her eyes.

His phone pinged. 'Lily,' they said in unison.

He dug it from his pocket and showed her what it said: Well?

Ella took the phone and typed back: He's not an idiot any more. He's perfect. Ella x.

With a chuckle he slipped it back into his pocket, before reaching down to retrieve her sandals. '*I'm not an idiot any more.* I think that's the best compliment I've ever received.'

She took the hand he held out towards her, and they strolled along the water's edge revelling in the moonlight and the stars.

'Something just occurred to me.'

She glanced up.

'Martin and Susie owe us big time. I mean, we *did* give them the wedding of the year.'

She blinked and then grinned. 'You're thinking that at some point in the future they have to return the favour?'

'Exactly! See?' He pointed at her, his eyes dancing. 'I always said we were on the same wavelength.'

Which of course meant she had to kiss him again. And then there was no more talking for a very long time.

* * * * *

If you enjoyed this story, check out these other great reads from Michelle Douglas

Secret Billionaire on Her Doorstep
Billionaire's Road Trip to Forever
Cinderella and the Brooding Billionaire
Escape with Her Greek Tycoon

All available now!